The Karma Hotel

The Karma Hotel

A Novel

Samineh I. Shaheem

"It's time to spread my wings and fly.
I surrender to my soul's power.
I will heat the universe with my fire,
And allow love to flower ..."

iUniverse, Inc.
New York Lincoln Shanghai

The Karma Hotel

iUniverse books may be ordered through booksellers or by contacting:

iUniverse
2021 Pine Lake Road, Suite 100
Lincoln, NE 68512
www.iuniverse.com
1-800-Authors (1-800-288-4677)

Because of the dynamic nature of the Internet, any Web addresses or links contained in this book may have changed since publication and may no longer be valid.

This is a work of fiction. All of the characters, names, incidents, organizations, and dialogue in this novel are either the products of the author's imagination or are used fictitiously.
Cover Image © 2007 by Salma Shaheem.
First English Edition Published in 2003.
Second English Edition Published in 2007.
Co-Edited by JV Delalunas.
Cover Image and Illustrations by Salma Shaheem.
Cover Design by Arezoo Rezaei Afsah.

ISBN: 978-0-595-47945-0 (pbk)
ISBN: 978-0-595-60758-7 (ebk)

Printed in the United States of America

Contents

* * * * * * * * * * * * *

We came whirling out of nothingness
scattering stars like dust.
The stars made a circle and in the middle we dance.
The wheel of heaven circles God like a mill.
If you grab a spoke, it will tear your hand off,
turning and turning it sunders all attachment
Were that wheel not in love it would cry 'enough'!
How long this turning?
Every atom turns bewildered.
Beggars circle tables, dogs circle carrion, the lover circles
his own heart
Ashamed, I circle shame.
A ruined water wheel whichever way I turn is the river.
If that rusty old sky creaks to a stop, still, still I turn.
And it is only God circling Himself.

* * * * * * * * * * * * *

Mawlana Jalal ad-Din Muhammad Rumi (1207-1273)
from Fragments—Ecstasies, translation by Daniel Liebert

Acknowledgments

To all the people who I have come into contact with during this life and all the other existences throughout time. I thank each of you for all the ways you have touched me.

This book is the work of forces beyond me, the writer, and thus speaks to you of its own accord—in places a narrator seems to know you, and understands things about the universe that lie beyond the grasp of individual writing. ***Please allow those personal conversations between you and I to penetrate deep into your thoughts as you read our story.***

A Message to The Person Holding Me ...

Dear Reader,

This will be quite a unique adventure for you, as it has been for me. I have found you for a reason, even though you might be thinking you found me instead. Either way, what's important is that an intricate set of events has led you to the exact place where you're now standing. Nothing is a coincidence, and thus no action should be devalued. There is always a lesson to be learned, a feeling to cherish, and most of all, an opportunity to perceive the world through different lenses and from different angles in every experience that comes our way.

I hope you'll take pleasure in embarking on this escapade with me in your hands. I hope I'll invite back thoughts from parts of your imagination that you had exiled to a far away place. I can only wish for you to wonder about some of the ideas that you'll come across. Help me accomplish my mission by putting a smile on your face, and perhaps I will make your heart skip a beat as we interact through this mystical journey.

I wish you love, happiness, and above all, an open mind with which to dance under a full moon, holding your soul mate till dawn.

Love,
This Book

Author's Note

Some people refer to it as the "Karma Hotel," others as the "center of enlightenment." In fact, there are many different names, a kaleidoscope of labels. Regardless of the title chosen for this unearthly location, whoever encounters the premises, whoever experiences a touch of its magic, will never again be the same. He and She will forever be transformed. Whether for better or worse, you decide. ***Perhaps you will even create a new name for our enchanted location.***

According to the doctrine of karma, for every morally determinate thought, word, or action, there will be corresponding karmic compensation—if not in this life, then in some future life. As can be found throughout various cultures and religions, and is specifically documented in many sacred texts, "As a man sows, so shall he reap." These actions can be quite mundane and of great force. In spite of their impact, they are accounted for and recorded on a designated level and dimension. You might compare this cosmic scenario to children in a classroom. The teacher acts as the higher being, observing and recording the behaviors of the children. If the students act according to the rules, they are rewarded. Similarly, they will be punished if they misbehave.

Yet there does not have to be a higher being on this mystical karmic plane or dimension, such as the teacher. There exists a force so strong, perhaps created by all the energies from the universe in synergistic combination, which keeps track of our rights and wrongs. These wrongs and rights can either be rewarded or punished in this life or in another life. However, the rewards or punishments are not as important as the lessons learned. These lessons are administered to provide our true selves with the means and desire to grow spiritually. In essence, these are the lessons of the universe as it blossoms in us and through us.

The growth process of wisdom and absolute love is experienced through many lifetimes, and these lifetimes transform, mold, and teach us how to live healthier lives. Through each experience and lesson learned, the soul has an opportunity to heal itself of past wounds in order to let go of hate and resentment, which act as obstacles in the way of spiritual progression. Often those events that bruised our very being in the distant past can influence present lives. The circle of life gives us a chance to return to those loose ends that need tying up; the circle that keeps going around and around, creating patterns, to prepare us for future incarnations.

By understanding the past patterns and trying to resolve issues that come our way, we can strive for a better present. These are the exact reasons that brought our four guests to "The Karma Hotel."

ℰℐ𝒞ℛℰℐ𝒞ℛℰℐ𝒞ℛℰℐ𝒞ℛ

The Guests

"'Tis just like a summer bird-cage in a garden: the birds that are without despair to get in, and the birds that are within despair and are in a consumption for fear they shall never get out."

—John Webster (*The White Devil, Act i. Sc. 2.*)

I'd like to introduce you to the four guests before we venture together to The Karma Hotel. In many ways, they are ordinary people just like you and I—however, they are also unique souls especially hand picked for this passage.

ဢ〜ᘓဢ〜ᘓဢ〜ᘓဢ〜ᘓ

Adriana

Adriana never really thought of herself as spiritual. In fact, she is someone who could be described as quite grounded, practical and living in the here and now. As a teenager, she would make fun of her sister for reading books from the spiritual or popular psychology section of the library. Adriana never understood her need for spiritual nourishment, nor did she think reading such "garbage," as she often called it, was a productive way of spending time.

It's amazing how certain events can totally alter our perception, remold our beliefs and open new doors of our thought process that we never even knew existed. Adriana experienced one of those life-altering encounters. After Nov. 3rd, she never laughed at her sister again and never mocked her for playing on a mystical field.

Adriana was invited to an office party. Everyone she worked with, which was most of the people she knew, attended. She was not seeing anyone at the time, and because she felt comfortable with most of the guests, she decided she did not need to drag her brother with her just for the sake of having a date. 'Poor guy', she thought. God knows he had stepped in "one too many times," as he would say, to accompany her to one of the sometimes boring, uptight gatherings for up and coming yuppies!

On this day, for some reason, Adriana felt special, happy with her life, content for being healthy. Not many people, including her, usually take the time to count their blessings for such mundane activities as "waking up" in the morning. We take so many little miracles, sent to us by the universe, for granted. Adriana decided to appreciate all that the "cosmos" (as her sister would say) had done for her. The world had smiled upon her and now it was time for her to smile back, and perhaps give it a hug! She took an extra long shower that day, immersing herself in the warmth of the water. Ever since she was a child, she occupied herself while bathing with a game she later called "The Symphony." She would stand under the shower, plug her ears with her fingers, and listen to the roar of water crashing down on her head. It almost sounds like being in a car during a thunderstorm, while listening to the rain rumbling down on the metal hood, but the sensation is much more powerful and intense.

Next time you're in the shower, try it my friend, it is an enlightening, exhilarating experience.

Adriana spent the rest of the day pampering herself and engaging in activities that she usually did not have time for anymore due to her busy schedule. Like calling old friends, writing emails, and later, going shopping with her mom. This was a day of appreciation for her existence, and appreciate she would.

She arrived at the party fashionably late but early enough to join in the fun before everyone got overly intoxicated. She looked at herself in the mirror before she walked in and decided she liked what she saw. Her nose could use a little lift, and perhaps she needed a haircut, but other than that, she knew she looked "hot" as some had said, and would continue to say. Adriana stood there for a moment, gazing at her reflection in the mirror. Her imagination suddenly shot back to one of her favorite fairy tales, *Snow White.* Adriana decided the mirror was enchanted and had all the answers.

"Mirror, Mirror on the wall, I know I'm not bad looking and I am quite a nice person, so where is my Prince Charming?" Adriana looked around to make sure no one had been witness to this moment of madness.

'Reality' soon called out to Adriana, beckoning her to forget about the mirror and she decided it was time to walk into the function hall. *Don't you wish you could get rid of 'reality' sometimes, dear reader? He's like the friend who thinks he knows it all—always there to dampen the mood and ruin all the fun; but very useful when you need advice or a jolt of honesty injected into denial.*

Nevertheless, Adriana's friend, 'Imagination', had not completely left her side. With every step she took, Adriana felt the weight of her words in front of the magic mirror. It was as if she had thrown a wish out into the universe, a wish that she did not even realize she wanted so desperately to come true, and was uncertain about the outcome. She decided to leave both 'reality' and 'imagination' at the door to fight it out amongst themselves. She had no desire for inner conflict tonight. This was time to dance!

It was at that precise moment that Adriana saw him. Was he a vision of beauty? No. Handsome perhaps, manly, tall, dark, and sophisticated looking, but he was by no means an Adonis. Nevertheless, he caught her eyes and stared back at her with equal intensity. For the first time in her life, she felt as if her soul were exposed. His eyes penetrated her being like no one else had ever done. She felt her legs weaken, and the ground beneath her feet steamed, seeming suddenly unstable. Is this what people mean when they say, "… he took my breath away?" she thought. A few minutes passed, or perhaps many minutes—she was not sure—and the feeling continued, but to a lesser extent, thank goodness, or else Adriana would have needed to sit down. She decided to break her gaze from this beautiful stranger, to start mingling with her colleagues.

"Hi Andrew. Am I glad to see you! Have you been here long?" Adriana tried to sound as casual as she possibly could, but she failed miserably.

"Hey gorgeous! Can I call you that or will you slap me with a sexual harassment case?"

Andrew leaned over and gave her a kiss on the cheek, took a sip from his drink, and then continued with a movement some tribes in Africa would call dancing.

"I should have done that a long time ago, to get rid of your corny self!"

They were buddies and always joked around, knowing they could without either of them taking any offence.

"Hey, who's that guy standing near the pillar? Does he work with us?"

Again Adriana's attempt at sounding casual failed. Andrew could sense her enthusiasm and immediately said, "That's my buddy Stephen. Let me introduce you."

Adriana was struck by those words like lightning and knew Fate had stepped in to make something happen. That 'something' is what brought Adriana to the "Karma Hotel."

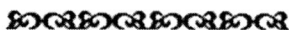

࿐ઉ૪ঙ৩ઉ૪ঙ৩ઉ૪ঙ৩ઉ૪ঙ৩

Daniel

Daniel's alarm clock went off at 5:30 as usual. You're probably thinking, 'he must be an early riser.' Unfortunately that was not the case; it was 5:30pm! Daniel hated the morning and had made a promise to himself never to wake up before late afternoon. He could hear the irritating buzz of his alarm clock beckoning him back to consciousness. How he had grown to despise that sound—the same sound that forced him awake to face another day, another miserable twelve hours before he could again run away from it all. He picked up his perceived torture device and smashed it against the wall. Regrettably, the abused clock was not silenced. It was as if Daniel had enraged the object, and now it wanted revenge. Due to the impact received, the dull buzzing sound turned into a high-pitched shriek. His only consolation was his bottle of apple juice next to his bed. Daniel loved the taste and the way it refreshed his thirst. He reached out for the juice and took a few big gulps. It was the same scenario, the same set of events that occurred almost everyday at 5:30pm, his hour of despair.

Daniel opened the curtains and saw the sun shining, the children of the neighborhood playing, Mr. Gordon, his neighbor watering his plants, and people just being 'people', going about their daily lives. Were they acting normal? Who decides what 'normal' is? He thought. Were the people he saw happy? Were they content to face another day? Did they ever stop to question this situation forced upon humanity called 'life'? Did they have aliens conducting experiments on them in the middle of grocery shopping? Daniel felt sorry for any hidden denial and repression. Deep down, buried somewhere in the soul of their souls, he was sure all people felt the same way he did.

He mused over the same question almost every waking moment of his existence. Frequent discussions would take place between his heart and mind about this matter. His heart would always try to see the emotional side of the situation, while his mind would take a more objective viewpoint. However, this dialogue was as productive as a priest trying to convert a Rabbi! Always ending at a dead end, always in stalemate, until some other distraction would separate the two and both would quiet momentarily. But unfortunately, such interludes were never long enough for the heart or mind to forget the issue at hand, and they would resume their debate at the first possible opportunity.

Daniel had been haunted by voices and dreams since his earliest memories. He couldn't have been more than 10 years old when his mother found him sitting in the middle of his room, his hands locked around his ears, screaming "LEAVE ME ALONE!!!"

She had heard him speaking aloud when playing with his toys alone, but she dismissed it as part of the game Daniel occupied himself with. She never gave it another thought. She remembered how she had had an imaginary friend when she was his age, someone she had created to play with her when her friends could not. What was wrong with that? Did we not all engage in make-believe situations as children? Was that not the fun part of being a child?

Unfortunately, that afternoon, the innocent interpretation of the situation by Daniel's mother was shattered by screams. Daniel's mother realized her son was no longer enjoying the 'imaginary friends'. On the contrary, they were tormenting him in a way that made her heart bleed. She spent many hours talking to him and praying to God to keep her son safe from evil spirits. She even blamed herself for not spending enough time with Daniel and for not having another child to help eliminate any need to create others to talk to. Daniel's mother questioned her every action as she was raising him. She provided him with all the privileges a young boy could ask for, and in a very functional and loving atmosphere. Where did she go wrong? Was his condition not meant to be for a child who had suffered abuse or had been raised in an improvised environment?

Many years passed and Daniel's situation worsened. He slowly became withdrawn from his family members, friends and classmates. He was a good student throughout elementary school; however, towards the end of grade 11, the quality of his schoolwork deteriorated enormously. His ambitions to become a doctor soon faded. How could he go to medical school when the thought of waking up in the morning was worse than death? Daniel would talk about soldiers following him, trying to convince him to join the army that was preparing to fight against 'the enemy' in World War IV. These soldiers had already fought and survived World War III and had many stories to tell. In addition, Daniel was pursued and head hunted by directors of various pharmaceutical companies that believed he held the cure for cancer. Of course, we also must not forget about the pink and blue colored beings from 'Marnus' (a combination of Mars and Venus) who routinely conducted experiments on him.

At first, Daniel's condition was labeled as depression and various other types of mood disorders. However, Daniel was careful not to reveal too much to psychologists during his sessions—in knowledge of all the strange medications which could be prescribed. Daniel would entertain himself by visualizing the look of shock on his shrink's face if he were to talk about the inhabitants of Marnus! He was still well enough to play the game, conscious and connected to reality enough to understand the probable repercussions he could face if he revealed too much about his condition. Daniel disclosed just enough information to fill up an hour with Dr. Hartley. He would usually answer direct questions in a very uninvolved and detached manner. Their meetings were in black and white, devoid of emotional coloring.

Daniel had memorized all of his psychiatrist's body language, like the way he nodded as he jotted down points about what his patient was saying. Daniel imagined Dr. Hartley making small doodles on his note pad or maybe even writing a 'to do' list of his errands for the following day. What good would it do to speak to someone anyway; he felt no one could begin to comprehend his state, especially a shrink! Was Dr. Hartley not a bit mad himself for choosing a profession in which one is required to understand the minds of 'disturbed' individuals? And if one such person truly is 'disturbed' or 'psychotic' in any way, why in the world should anyone believe anything he or she says?!

Keep thinking about these questions, my cosmic traveler, for you may hold the answers.

Regrettably, Daniel was not always in control of his moods or actions. One warm summer night, after many hours of drinking, and continuous arguments with Teremanga (the ruler of Marnus), anger engulfed him. He lashed out at everything and everyone around him. He broke things within his reach and smashed most of the windows of his family's small house with a baseball bat. Daniel's poor mother had no other choice but to call the police, who arrived just in time to interrupt his rampage before he started in on the furniture.

That night Daniel was taken to jail to "unwind", to spend a day or two thinking about his actions. He sat in the confines of his cold jail cell. Suddenly a feeling of comfort and security came over him. The sensation was very instinctual and natural. The jail no longer seemed dirty and destitute; nothing like what he had thought a jail cell would feel like at all. In Daniel's mind, his bleak surroundings somehow transformed into his mother's womb; making him feel warm, sheltered, nourished and unperturbed. Soon after, he fell into a deep sleep—the kind of sleep that we do not want to wake up from because of the intense relaxation and peace accompanying it, sometimes overwhelming us.

When was the last time you experienced such a sensation? Perhaps it has been too long. It was through the dreams Daniel had that night that he eventually came to the "Karma Hotel."

ဆဝ၁ဆဝ၁ဆဝ၁ဆဝ၁

Alexander

Now Alexander is a different type of being, not one of the Earthly kind. A rare human, with so much love and compassion, that at times he would be mistaken as a push over or as being too gullible. He exhibited these traits right from the age of 5 or 6. He always shared his toys and never instigated a fight with friends. On the contrary, he was the one who would be the peace-maker, always stepping in to iron out issues between people. He would spend hours trying to persuade his loved ones to give rather than to take, to appreciate and hope to understand others instead of trying to enforce opinions and ideology onto them.

Please do not misunderstand Alexander. He is not under the false impression that we are all good or that evil can be permanently erased from the face of the Earth. He does not want to take it upon himself to alter the decrepit and failing morals of our species. But he does believe in one thing: if we give a lost soul a chance, that soul will be found. If we show compassion to someone cruel, then the cruelty may be slowly replaced by kindness. Not to imply that any individual is intrinsically benevolent, but if one sees that we perceive him and her as caring, then perhaps that connection will open the door to their hearts—aiding each of us in our choices to be caring. There must be a starting point for everyone, right?

Alexander's level of mysticism and spirituality far exceed the Christian commandments or dictated ways of life through any organized religion. Actually, Alexander never cared too much for organized religion—he believes it divides people rather than bringing them together. Religion serves its purpose, sure, and all three of the major religions first came to people and societies who were debatably in dire need of stricter codes of conduct being enforced upon them; however, Alexander hated the idea that people behaved or were moral accordingly with a belief that they may be judged and perhaps sent to burn in hell for eternity. Does not this motive of virtue contradict everything 'religion' is about? Are we decent respectable beings because we fear the Day of Judgment, or do we behave morally because we still have faith in humanity as being habitually righteous, in giving to others as they have given to us?

You may want to think about these questions a little bit more carefully before you answer. Ponder them each day of your lifetime, perhaps. That is what Alexander decided to do.

Alexander believes in altruism, he lives his life performing favors, little miracles, or good deeds without expecting anything in return from the recipients. It would only be a bonus if the Universe noticed and She decided to reward him in some fashion. And She often did. The Universe smiled with Alexander on more than one occasion when he needed to be acknowledged. This satisfied him enormously and is enough motivation to convince him that his spiritual beliefs are more than simply earnest, despite the fact that others believe him to be a fool.

Unfortunately, the Universe would occasionally forget about Alexander too—or so it seemed. Not in a drastic fashion as in allowing episodes of tragedy to descend upon him, but in a much more "subtle way," as he would say. He would have periods of intense exhaustion during which he felt absolutely drained, for example. Sometimes days would pass before he felt enough energy to get out of bed. He would feel as if he were carrying the weight of the world on his shoulders.

Such occurrences would leave as suddenly as they arrived. He called them his "unwelcome visitors". Have you ever known someone who, although you may care for them deeply, has an aura or energy so heavy that after a few hours with them you're ready to hibernate for the next 20 hours? In a way, Alexander's episodes of exhaustion were like the effects our 'heavy friends' have on our soul. The only difference for Alexander was that he could neither control nor fully foresee his meetings with this feeling. These episodes struck at the oddest times—while taking a shower, stuck in traffic and early in the morning. However, what Alexander did know was that they usually followed after spending extended periods of time with certain family members and friends.

Alexander's family was very worried about this problem, especially his mother. She made appointments for him to see numerous doctors. Of course, being the special soul that he is, Alexander never wanted to disappoint or worry her at all. So he would show up on time to meet the physicians, ranging from the family doctor to the individuals working in phytotherapy (medical herbs). They would poke and prod him, take every possible sample and ask him endless lists of questions. He was so used to the routine by now that he would tell a new doctor, "You forgot to take a urine sample. Don't you need one?"

Unfortunately no amount of urine or blood was sufficient for any of these doctors to correctly diagnose Alexander. He would watch the needle of the syringe being injected into his vein, and be amazed at the way his blood would fill up the tube, so red, such a sign of life. Yet ironically, these people who were supposed to be helping him were, in a crazy way, draining him of his soul. Imagine watching more than 60 of those little tubes being filled with your blood? Each doctor would have different ideas about what was happening to him, and each was quite proud of formulating his or her theory. However, there was never any relevance to Alexander's condition in their suppositions, which were highly insignificant and inaccurate.

Until one day, Alexander decided to take matters into his own hands. He was completely frustrated by the dead-end responses he was getting, all the useless medication he was being prescribed, and wasting his time and energy repeating his symptoms to people who might as well have been the local butcher! On this day, he found a flyer someone had placed on his windshield. The leaflet was beautifully decorated and written on ancient looking paper. It was a psychic advertising her abilities and claiming *"… to have all the answers to your questions."*

Alexander was immediately intrigued. Not that this was the first time he went to see a psychic. Oh no, he had been to at least half a dozen of them. Remember, he was the child of 'Spirituality'—but somehow, this was going to be different, and somehow he knew it would be different. The paper felt like it had found a home in his hands. Alexander looked around at all the other parked cars and none of them had a flyer on their windshield—he recognized an omen when he saw one. Alexander also respected the message and knew he had to contact "Alba". His meeting with Alba and the events that followed are what brought this unique soul to the "Karma Hotel."

••••••••

Jennifer

Think about a time in which you felt a sense of belonging or familiarity in a place visited for the first time. With that thought in mind, you will relate closely to our next guest Jennifer.

Jennifer was 9 years old when she first went to Austria. Her parents had never been there and thought it might be a nice vacation spot for the family. Jennifer was always the curious one, the one intrigued by whatever she encountered, and she was excited at the thought of embarking on a new adventure.

On their way from the airport to the hotel, she stared out of the taxi window, taking in all the new sights and sounds of this new world. Her parents were quite amused at her interest in Austria and wondered what she was thinking as they observed her making mental notes regarding her surroundings.

As soon as they checked into the hotel, Jennifer turned to her mother and said, "I've missed this place so much. Why didn't we come back here before?"

Jennifer looked straight at her mother and eagerly awaited a reply. Her mother was so shocked and bewildered about Jennifer's comment that she thought she had misheard or misunderstood the child. So she asked for clarification by saying, "what did you say honey? What do you mean you missed this place so much? It's the first time we've been here!"

"Oh mother, you always treat me like a baby; I know we used to live here. Will we visit our old house?"

At this point Jennifer's mother was unsure about how she should react. She carefully selected her words, dismissed her daughters comment as another one of her 'little jokes' and decided to go along with it.

"Yes, we might do that. It would be interesting to see who's living there now, don't you think?"

She watched her daughter's reaction to see if her words had satisfied her. Indeed they had, for Jennifer took what her mother had said very seriously.

"Great! I think we should buy some flowers for the people living there before we visit."

Jennifer started unpacking her suitcase, thinking aloud about all the other escapades she wanted to go on while in Austria.

Her mother soon forgot Jennifer's strange comment and went about her own unpacking. However, the issue was not laid to rest just yet. Throughout their stay, Jennifer did not stop mentioning the fact that she was sure they used to live there and would ask to visit their old home at every opportunity. Jennifer's cries of curiosity were rarely acknowledged.

Parents are very good at brushing aside subjects that are difficult to explain or have no place in a rational or logical world. Somehow, the ability to dream, to imagine, eludes us as we get older and become caught up in the day-to-day realities of life—as in a web. Jennifer's commentary had no place in her parents' world, nor did either of them want to open the door to such thoughts. Both her mother and father vigilantly discarded their daughter's insistence about living there before and tried to distract her with other activities.

Jennifer eventually stopped her demands because she came to realize that her parents did not understand. The family returned home a week later, but Jennifer's thoughts remained on Austria. She grew up never forgetting her experience. She had always been fascinated by far away places, but no other location had a greater impact on her than Austria.

In college, she was drawn to anyone from Europe, especially if they were Austrian or had ever been there. Her friends and family members were also aware of her curious fascination and would joke with her about finding her a mail-order groom from that side of the Atlantic. She would humor them and let them make fun of her, but deep down inside she believed in what she felt and knew—that the time would come when she would return to that land to visit her old home. This journey would occur many years later with the assistance of the "Karma Hotel", but not as she could ever imagine.

Daniel, Jennifer, Adriana and Alexander were contacted at different times, dear seeker. They all went through different experiences leading them to the Karma Hotel. They were chosen mostly because of their desire and hunger to know more about the happenings in their lives, and because Earthly and practical explanations were not sufficient. Nevertheless, the time in which each was ready for the Karma Hotel was astoundingly identical.

ෂ෮෫෮ෂ෮෫෮ෂ෮෫෮ෂ෮෫෮

The Place

"*If you have built castles in the air, your work need not be lost; that is where they should be. Now put the foundations under them.*"

—Henry David Thoreau (*Walden*)

The hotel building looked far from observable from the outside. Nestled between two mountains, the Karma Hotel seemed as if it were carved out of the surrounding landscape, molded from the rocks and the soil it rested upon. The trees and the bushes embraced the enormous edifice so tightly that it was difficult to see the building through the dense vegetation. Only after careful inspection did the dilapidated and ancient structure peep through slightly at any observer.

The plant life was absolutely breathtaking. There were trees and flowers that visitors had never seen before: so many colors and shapes, so many different types of blossoms, as far as the eye could see. Each of these unique flowers had released their scent into the air, creating the most fragrant atmosphere—a delicious mixture of vanilla, jasmine and apricot.

The four guests, Daniel, Adriana, Alexander, and Jennifer stared in awe. They knew they were being taken to a mysterious and magical location; however, none of them could have ever anticipated this extraordinary view. It was truly an awesome sight, and they were astounded by the delicious taste of the air they breathed. The scent affected Adriana the most. *Is it not truly magical the way a particular fragrance can carry us to another time and place, recreating the scene, the mood, and the people involved, all with the hint of a familiar aroma? Reader, which perfume or cologne do you relate to your first love? I believe you have still kept the bottle, is that so?*

Adriana did. She had kept everything Stephen ever gave her. Each article was a sacred object of their affection. One of her favorite gifts was a perfume he had given her. During that particular meeting, they had spent the afternoon together, talking, eating, and making love. She couldn't get enough of him and desperately wanted time to stop when they were together. Stephen was her dream lover, too good to be true. She ached for him even at that moment. *But when something seems too good to be true, it probably is not, right?*

The answer does not have to be a simple one, and the lessons learned certainly are not easy. The question is not whether something is true or untrue, but more about the reasons and obstacles that stand in the way of perfection. In Adriana's situation, it was Stephen's wife.

She closed her eyes, inhaled another deep breath of the fragrant air, and recalled the way they had been lying in bed, both on their sides, face to face, soul to soul. He grabbed the bottle of exquisite perfume from his side, took off the top and started splashing the scent all over her naked body. The feeling of the cold liquid on her skin was so exhilarating that it took her breath away. But that did not stop Stephen, nor did her playful cries for him to stop his crazy game. It was as if this erotic scene had hypnotized him. A heavenly juice soaked his lover's beautiful body that glistened in the light, and the scent of jasmine and rose danced around them. Passion engulfed the entire room, leaving no room for inhibitions.

The present rudely interrupted Adriana's beautiful daydream and she was suddenly taken by everyone's stillness. She looked around and it was as if they were all in a trance. None of them had uttered a word since the beginning of their journey. Each was in his or her own imaginary worlds, reminiscing about various events that this environment had evoked in them as they stared up at the hotel. So Adriana decided it was time to break the silence.

"Can you believe your eyes? This looks like something out of a fairytale! … Wow, is it real? It looks more like an image rather than a real building. Let's touch it! C'mon guys, what are we waiting for?"

Jennifer's curiosity had gotten the best of her and it was time to do some investigating.

"I knew places like this existed!" She replied to Adriana's topic starter, "I feel so sorry for anyone who's forgotten how to dream! Thank you Fate for bringing us all here."

"Ahhhh," Alexander accentuated, forever grateful, forever appreciative for all the miracles of life.

"Let me know when you're done so I can throw up!" said Daniel.

Adriana looked at him and could not help but giggle. A part of her agreed with what Daniel was saying.

"'Thank you Fate'?!?! Forgetting how to dream?!?!'" Are you for real man?"

Alexander was exactly the type of person Daniel despised. 'A self righteous—head-in-the clouds-flower-picking moron who helps old ladies across the road!' Yes, he knew the type and could not stand to breathe the same air as this sanctimonious being. How in the world could he hide his unhappiness so well? Or maybe the question should be 'why' in the world does he hide his unhappiness and instead choose to sugar coat it with this air of morality?

"Yes I am for real Daniel, and maybe the two of us could learn a thing or two from each other. Now would that be so terrible?"

Alexander felt his heart tug at Daniel's seemingly lost soul. Daniel was so bitter, so angry with everyone and everything.

Jennifer immediately wondered what Daniel's story was. She was amused in a way, intrigued at the differences between the two men who had accompanied them. Like the good psychologist that she 'hoped' to one day be, she started piecing the story of Daniel's life together. *Just as I'm sure you have already done about these four interesting people. I wonder how close your deductions will be to that of Jennifer's about Daniel. Let's ask her.*

Jennifer had seen the likes of Daniel before: probably abused as a child, from a broken home—maybe a high school drop out blaming the rest of the world for his failures. His dysfunctional family life had probably scared him emotionally. He was constantly projecting his anger onto other people, a typical defense mechanism employed to deal with his internal turmoil and anxiety. Anything bad that happened to him was always someone else's fault, or perhaps caused by being unlucky. How much further from the truth could Jennifer have been about Daniel?

"Please hold hands in a circle and let the process begin," Arya interrupted Jennifer's thoughts, Chaperoning.

Ayra had not spoken to the four guests until that moment. No one could figure out where he was from. He had an accent but not an identifiable one. He fit the whole environment perfectly. He was so mystifying and so ambiguous.

Alexander was the first to assume the requested position, and followed by Jennifer. Adriana and Daniel were the two skeptics of the group. They hesitated at first, but then joined their travel companions in the circle.

"Yeah, let the process begin. Let's all hug, kiss each other and bond. That will make it all better! Can this get any cornier?!"

Daniel was already starting to regret accepting this invitation. What good would it do anyway? This was 'probably like one of those hippie retreats in the woods where people would embrace and cry all weekend long. They would all then return to their lives with more issues than they started out with!'

Just then, one of the inhabitants of Marnus suddenly appeared next to Daniel.

"Daniel! How dare you betray us by joining another group of extraterrestrials? You signed the contract of loyalty, remember?"

"I don't have time for you right now. Leave me alone!"

Arya thought Daniel was talking to him and decided it was time to deal with this rebellious creature who was starting to affect the group's energy.

"Daniel, its time to join us. Please ground yourself. Your energy is all over the place and it's interfering with the process of initiation."

Daniel managed to get himself under control and the group commenced with the first step of the journey that would change each of them forever.

Arya uttered a chant under his breath. He whispered it so discreetly that the rest of the group, holding hands in the tight circle, could barely hear. It was in an unfamiliar ancient language. Nevertheless, the words impacted them all. Without comprehending the language, all of them felt the profound emotional meaning Arya's words encapsulated, like reading a deep and complicated poem about love translated from another language. You may not understand the details of the verse; however, the tears that well up in your eyes clearly signify how much you've been touched by the words.

Daniel was first to feel the force. It was evident in his face and the way his shoulders suddenly relaxed—his posture gradually becoming at ease. Like a wave, that energy passed through each of them, having a similar effect as it traveled through each atom of their being. Why had Arya chosen Daniel for the power to touch first? Because Daniel was the most unenthusiastic of the bunch and he wanted to make sure the preliminary burst of the energy should spread through him before it weakened as it gradually moved towards Adriana, Jennifer, and last but not least, Alexander.

This process took less than five minutes, but it felt like a lifetime. Arya's energy passed through the group, and as each person held hands with another—each person had flashbacks of their lives. A summary of their time on earth was projected in their minds, and perfectly formulated clips of important events unraveled before them.

Did Daniel see his demons? Were Jennifer's images of Austria? Did Adriana see her beloved? And Alexander, did he envisage saving humanity's essence? I know you're curious, but patience my freethinking spirit. You will not be disappointed.

Everyone in the group took time opening their eyes; Arya did not want to rush them. He wanted them to savor the moment, to be overwhelmed and taken by the rapture that the initiation process entailed. He had a look of pride in his eyes, a feeling of yet another successful session with four strangers. Never had he failed to bring down the defenses of the most unresponsive guest, like Daniel, who looked like a new man—with only a glow sweeping over his face. The energy was just too pure, too powerful and forever healing to fail.

"Alright my travelers, thank you for opening your hearts to our first step in the process. Please take your belongings and let's proceed inside," said Arya.

Adriana, Daniel, Jennifer and Alexander grabbed their small suitcases. In the invitation that arrived at each member's mailbox, they were told not to trouble themselves with too many possessions, to come with only a few necessities. The Karma Hotel would provide everything they needed. Arya watched the four guests. As they walked towards the entrance of the hotel, he took mental notes about how each of the four guests looked, the expressions on their faces and their over all energy. They seemed so much more grounded, comfortable in their environment after the initiation. Well, all except Adriana.

"Mr. Arya, you haven't really told us where we're going or what to expect. Could you give us a brief rundown of the agenda for the next few days?"

Adriana knew the others were thinking the same thing and decided to again nominate herself as a spokes-person for the group.

"My sweet Adriana, I appreciate your impatience and your desire to have a more concrete schedule for this journey. However, this is neither a board meeting at your company nor a weekend getaway booked at Smith's Travel Agency. The truth—or 'the agenda'—as you have chosen to call it, will disentangle gradually."

Arya looked at each guest for an equal amount of time as he delivered his sermon.

"It will be different for each of you and the uniqueness of this experience will make all the mystery, all of your lack of comprehension and trepidation at this moment, seem worthwhile very soon. I only ask you to trust me, to trust us at The Karma Hotel, the same way that we trusted you enough to invite you here. So without further adieux, please follow me inside. We're running late and there are people waiting to welcome you."

Arya felt that one more exercise would benefit this group, since Adriana's question had disturbed their tranquility.

"One last word of advice: leave your insecurities, defenses, and any other reservations created for the real world out in this beautiful garden. Take a deep breath, the deepest one of your lives, and when you exhale, visualize these emotions escaping your soul."

Daniel welcomed this suggestion wholeheartedly. For the first time in his life, he was beginning to feel excited and motivated about doing something even though he was not yet ready to admit this new sensation to the others.

Jennifer felt like she was high—high on life, high on this experience, and totally intoxicated by the fragrant air. Alexander was quite taken by Arya. He thought that this individual had the most rewarding job, to be able to make a difference in people's lives. He wondered if the hotel was accepting applications; perhaps they had a position open for him.

The path leading up to the door was laid in a beautiful brown and beige marble, smooth and absolutely flawless. Adriana felt as if she were Dorothy from the *Wizard of Oz*. She looked down at her shoes and noticed that she had worn red sandals. Adriana decided Daniel was the cowardly lion, Alexander the Tin Man, Jennifer the Straw Man and Arya was the wizard. She looked up at the skies to see if she could spot the wicked witch flying on a broomstick.

From a distance, the door of the hotel seemed hidden by all the ivy embracing it; however, it became more visible as they approached it. What an impressive entrance. The doors must have been at least 20 feet high and 10 feet wide, in solid wood, and it held the most intricate and detailed carvings. The door looked to be hundreds of years old. As they got closer, the words woven into the carving soon became apparent. Each guest stood still for a moment to read the inscription:

Enter And You Shall Be Forever Enlightened

What a wonderful and inviting set of letters. How exhilarating and pleasurable to begin a transformation process with such words opening the door for you. Arya stepped in front of Jennifer, who was the closest one to the door. She needed to touch the words, trace her fingers along the letters, as if each letter possessed a power to somehow touch her back.

Arya took out a brass key and slipped it into a hidden keyhole. He closed his eyes and chanted a few sentences under his breath. He then turned the key, three times to the left and twice to the right. The guests waited anxiously. They couldn't wait to see what secrets were being stored within the walls of such a huge and picturesque structure.

The massive doors began to open, with no effort put forth by Arya. He had taken the key out and simply nudged one side forward. Alexander thought his heart was going to jump out of his chest from excitement while Jennifer's impatience burned through her like a heat flash. Adriana was waiting to be dazzled, and Daniel was trying to construct the interior of the hotel in his mind in order to compare the scene that was about to unravel before them with his expectations.

Just as they were about to enter, a beautiful and slender woman appeared in front of them. She had the softest voice, the sweetest smile and the warmest disposition any of them had ever beheld. The gown she was wearing was breathtaking. Scarlet velvet fabric embroidered with pearls and garnet embraced her body, draping all the way to the ground. Her movements were fluid yet sure. She was a celestial vision in so many ways that the Gods, if asked, were sure to claim her as one of them.

"Welcome, my travelers. It has been so long since I've seen you all, each one in another life. Alexander, remember when we were working in the diamond mine together? Daniel, what a laugh it was to be a fellow clown with you in the most famous circus in Moscow, ahhhhh … so long ago.

"Jennifer, you look so similar to when I knew you, as my mother, three lives ago. And Adriana, I hope you're nicer in this life than you were in the last one. You so unfairly picked on us everyday during class!" She spoke so causally, making small talk regarding such events.

Daniel, Adriana, Jennifer and Alexander looked at each other, not knowing what to say in response. They were shocked and turned to Arya for an explanation of the words that this beautiful stranger had just released upon their first meeting. Arya quickly came to their rescue to ease the obvious discomfort his colleague had caused.

"Dear guests, I'd like you to meet Rhea. She is what we call 'the chief guidance counselor.' Now is this anyway to greet our guests Rhea? You've scared the poor souls with your opening speech!"

"Were you joking? I wasn't your mother in a past life, was I?" Jennifer needed some clarification; she had already been deeply confused, even before entering the hotel.

"No, my sweet child, I was joking. I apologize for startling you with my whimsical greeting. I often find it helps to break the ice with my clients. I also secretly enjoy shocking you into your first encounter with thinking about your past missions." Rhea winked at Arya as she revealed a naughty side of her respectable demeanor.

"Welcome, we've been waiting for you. You must all be so tired after your journey. Please allow me to show you to your rooms."

Rhea further pushed the opening door of the hotel to release and started walking through the entrance. The inside of the hotel looked like a continuation of the beautiful garden outside. There were trees, plants and the same exotic flowers scattered everywhere. It was almost as if the vegetation had decided to seek refuge within the confines of the building, creeping and crawling its way through the main lobby. Only all was more manicured and orderly compared to the wild and natural state of the garden outside.

There were more large doors like the one they had entered through at opposite ends of every wall. Each was more lavishly decorated than the one before it, not in terms of colour—but also in shape, size and the material that the door was composed of.

We'll come back to those doors soon my free thinker, for they play a crucial role in our guests' journeys.

The only furniture visible was six hammocks hanging at different locations in the lobby. 'Hammocks? What odd furniture to display in a hotel lobby'—that's exactly what the four individuals were thinking as Rhea led them through the foyer. These were not your usual hammocks either. Each one was decorated with different ornaments and varied in color and size. These were not like the flimsy hammocks in one of our relative's homes that throw us off the minute we try to rest in one.

The hammocks at The Karma Hotel looked so inviting, so comfortable. Adriana was tempted to try one out, but decided she would be a conformist in this situation and follow the rest of the group. Boring, true, but sometimes a much better resolution comes about when the appropriateness of time and place meet. The place was right, but it was not the right time for any of them to lounge in the powerful vessels they knew as hammocks. They would know better later.

The four guests walked slowly and cautiously, observing their new environment. Daniel was thinking about how different the entrance was compared to the image he had conjured up in his mind while walking towards the building. He had imagined antique furniture displayed throughout, rare and expensive paintings, lavish materials draped around the windows, somewhat like the hotels he had stayed in with his parents while vacationing in Paris.

Rhea escorted them to an elevator. They entered single file, waiting for either Rhea or Arya to give them further instructions about what to do or where to go. At this point, Arya said his good byes, promised he'd see the group later, and walked off to the opposite end of the lobby.

"Isn't he wonderful? He's been working with us for more than 312 years; I don't know what we'd do without him!" Rhea giggled as she talked about Arya.

"Now was that a joke as well, Rhea? You need to warn us about these comments you throw around. We really don't know what to expect!"

Alexander wanted to reach out and hug this beautiful creature. He was in awe of her grace, and at the same time so taken by her humor.

"It seems you're used to me already, Alexander. There should always be time for jokes and pleasure, don't you think my friends? Life would be so bland if we were serious all the time."

"I agree," said Jennifer "I think I'm going to love this place!"

Daniel listened to Rhea talking about her philosophy of life, love and fun. He wished so much that he could inject some of those ideas in his way of life. Maybe things would change for him after this experience. Maybe he would be able to look forward to waking up everyday. Maybe he would be able to take a walk in the park and enjoy the same things as others inhabiting the planet. Maybe it was time for him to open his heart and mind to living. After all, what could he lose? Yet, there was so much to gain.

The group went up to the 1st floor, the doors opened and Rhea asked Daniel to step outside.

"You'll be staying on this floor. Your room is around the corner, you can't miss it. There's only one room on each floor. Get some rest, settle yourself in and there will be someone visiting you in a little while."

The same procedure followed for Adriana staying on the 2nd floor, Jennifer on the 3rd floor and Alexander on the 4th floor.

Their rooms were huge, so spacious and comfortable. Each room had items that were tailored to meet the occupant's individual needs. Daniel found his mini bar filled with his favorite drink, apple juice. Adriana found a closet full of beautiful nightgowns, in different colors and materials. She felt as if her Fairy God Mother had granted her first wish. Jennifer's desk was covered with books about different countries and cultures. How she loved to read and escape to these places in her mind. Alexander immediately threw himself onto the massive bed in the middle of the room. It must have been the biggest, most comfortable bed he had ever laid on.

Rhea went back down to her study. She called Arya to her office to have a chat about her new guests.

"Aren't they a delightful bunch, Arya? Did you have a chance to get to know them on your way to the hotel?"

Rhea looked at him intently for any important information he might want to disclose about their visitors.

"Well, you know Rhea; we try not to say too much on the way. It kills the element of surprise and mystery. Anyhow, questions regarding guest experiences at the hotel always direct the conversation and curiosity takes over their minds. So, as usual, I left them to create their own scenarios and meditate on whatever matter was occupying their thoughts at the time."

She looked pleased with his answer, but he knew he should give her some more input about the vibes he had picked up during initiation.

"They all seem very nice and genuine. Of course a little bit of anxiety is expected considering the nature of their trip. I must warn you about Daniel. He seems the most obstinate of the bunch. We may have a bit of difficulty breaking down his defenses. He gives the impression that he's been through many different and perhaps unsuccessful conventional methods of healing."

"Yes, I gathered that from my brief encounter with him. Poor soul. I'll let Dameer know before he meets him."

Dameer was the in-house psychiatrist. Each of the four guests will soon have the pleasure of making his acquaintance.

"What about Alexander? I get the feeling he's one of us, or perhaps was at one time."

"I think you might be right. He's very kind, a very important member of the group."

"Alright Arya, thank you again for a job well done. I'll keep you informed about them all as we progress. See you later."

Rhea got up, hugged Arya and watched him as he left her study. She felt the same sense of excitement as she did with all the new members that came her way. The thrill of her work only amplified with each assignment. She thought about all the sad souls that woke up each morning to meaningless jobs they hated, to relationships that drained them, to troubles that were all they could see. How she longed to be able to reach out to them all, to bring essence back to their lives and wake them up to a fuller life. She consoled the pain in her heart by reminding herself that she could only do so much. She could not carry the responsibility and the burden of those people who chose to remain asleep.

ᏠᏣᏣᏐᏠᏣᏣᏐᏠᏣᏣᏐᏠᏣᏣᏐ

The Personnel

"One certainly has a soul; but how it came to allow itself to be enclosed in a body is more than I can imagine. I only know if once mine gets out, I'll have a bit of a tussle before I let it get in again to that of any other."

—Lord Byron *(Byron's Letters & Journals, vol. 5)*

Rhea gave her guests a few hours to recover from their journey. She knew they were tired, but at the same time anxious to know more about the workings of the Karma Hotel. When she felt the time more appropriate, Rhea would call each one of the four guests individually, inviting them to meet her in the lobby.

Relaxing in her room, Adriana looked outside of the huge window before her. As she watched the sun setting, she remembered all the times she and Stephen had been witness to this miraculous event: the ending of a day and the beginning of a night. She wondered what he was doing, if he was at home with his wife and children, playing with them, perhaps making love to her. She felt her stomach knot at the thought, then felt guilty for allowing herself to feel that way. After all, that was his wife and they had every right to enjoy the pleasures of an intimate relationship.

Adriana thought aloud, "So why does he keep coming back to me? What does he want from me?" Adriana had asked Stephen this question directly on many occasions. He would take her into his arms and say, "EVERYTHING … every square inch of your heart, body, mind and soul." Stephen's response however spurred new questions: was he giving her 'EVERYTHING'? Or was he simply using her as a way to fill all the voids of his own heart?

The phone interrupted her thoughts.

"Adriana, its Rhea here. We'll be expecting you in the lobby in five minutes."

"Alright Rhea, I'll be there. See you soon," Adriana replied, just before hanging up the phone. Maybe the phone call was a sign that her questions would soon be answered.

Meanwhile, Jennifer was so taken by all the interesting books left for her that she did not know which one to concentrate on.

All of them contained fascinating pictures and information—but she was inevitably drawn to one about Austria. As she flipped through the pages, some of the pictures of Vienna, the capital, looked familiar. However, as Jennifer had not been there since she was so young, she did not recall too many details. Yet her dreams of the place still occurred quite frequently, getting even more vivid as she got older. The perplexing and frustrating part was that she knew the place in her dreams was Austria and the characters were familiar to her although she could not say definitively that she knew them.

Whatever the circumstance in the dreams, Jennifer felt an unambiguous sense of belonging—but without remembering any real details after waking up, it was not feasible to decipher any possible messages. Jennifer felt that she had spent too long wondering without getting any answers. She thought how things would be different here at the Karma Hotel. For the first time she felt comfortable knowing that her search for this mysterious connection might not end in vain. She received a call from Rhea informing her about the meeting. Jennifer grabbed her handbag and headed for the elevator.

Comfortably positioned, Alexander did not want to leave the bed he rested in. He felt he could sleep forever, sleep the most restful and peaceful sleep imaginable. At the same time, he was too anxious, too excited to waste time lying down. He thought about all the people whom he had love for, all of whom he would like to share this magical and exciting journey he was about to embark on.

He did not care what the outcome would be; he was more interested in what he would learn, in the process of encountering such a unique place. Was that not enough? The thought of knowing that a place like the Karma Hotel actually existed, that the people here devoted their lives to making other people's lives that much more worth living, gave him hope—which was all but a new sensation to him. Just then, the phone rang. It was Rhea, speaking as if she had read his thoughts.

"Hi Alexander, I know you're relaxing on the best bed in the house, but I must ask you to part with it for awhile. I'll be expecting you in the lobby in five minutes."

Alexander thought Rhea's voice was the most soothing he had ever heard.

"Yes, I'm very comfortable, thank you. But I'll be there right away."

He hung up, and headed for the elevator.

For the first time in a very long time, Daniel did not want to drink apple juice. He reflected upon whether or not such habits were just another part of his 'messed up personality'. The fact that he did not crave his favorite drink which was available in abundance at this moment, provoked him to question if he was rebelling yet again, 'being a stubborn difficult jerk'.

No, he decided it was much deeper than that, that there must be a much more positive explanation. Somehow, apple juice, the drink that would aid him to face the day, was not required here. He felt a level of content and did not need to limit himself to just one type of beverage. Why not try some other drink? How about cranberry or pineapple juice? Daniel waited for one of the voices to answer as they so often did when he posed questions to himself. However, no one spoke to him, no one suggested any plan of action or choices he should make. How amazing to be able to enjoy the silence.

Up until the phone rang. It was, of course, the beautiful and funny Rhea. Daniel recalled what she had said about past lives in the corridor and thought about the possibility of working with her in a circus. He was not sure whether she had been kidding, even if she said she was. Maybe in that life his situation was reversed. He was a clown, supposedly a happy character, but he could have been the most miserable and sad person inside.

Maybe he had used up all his happiness, and therefore he was not able to hide any of his miseries in this life. He decided he was reading way too much into what Rhea said; 'it was only a joke Daniel', he said to himself, 'lighten up for God's sake!' Rhea then asked him to meet her and the others in the lobby. He put away some of his belongings into the closet and headed for the elevator.

Each of the guests arrived within a few minutes of one another. Rhea met them in front of the elevator as she had promised. She had changed her clothes and was now wearing a beautiful red velvet evening gown. She looked truly stunning. They exchanged comments about their rooms, spoke about the splendor and extravagance, and compared notes with reference to the special items placed to meet their individual needs.

Rhea asked her guests to follow her across the lobby. They turned and followed her towards one of the doors that was on the left-hand wall. This door was made mostly of different colored glass. Daniel thought about whether or not he had seen this door when they had arrived. Was it there before? He must have missed it.

"I would like you to meet the rest of the members of our little family here. As I'm sure you've noticed, the Karma Hotel is a calm and tranquil place, and you won't find many people parading around. Nor will you encounter any other activities other than the tasks you'll be engaging in as a necessary part of your experience here."

Rhea weighed her words carefully so that her comments would not reveal too much too soon. She then took out a set of keys from the pocket of her gown. She opened the massive glass door and invited the four visitors to enter.

The room seemed fairly empty, void of too much furniture, yet it offered a very warm feeling, in the emotional sense of the word. The walls were painted bright yellow and the floor was covered in rich cherry wood. The main piece of furniture in the room was a huge, solid and thick dining table—revealing the most gorgeous and elaborate carvings all over its surface and up the length of its legs. The table was large enough to comfortably seat 20 people. Arya was seated on one side, and the head of the table was vacant, presumably left for Rhea. There were four more individuals present.

"Dear colleagues, Id like to introduce our visitors to you. This is Daniel, Jennifer, Adriana and Alexander," Rhea beamed with pride, as if she were introducing her own children to distant relatives.

"Please take a seat," she said to her guests, "We like to make the introductions as informal as we possibly can. You've met Arya and now I'd like you to meet the others."

Rhea stood behind one of the seated women.

"This is Chance. She's our psychic here at the Karma Hotel. Chance, remind me to change that title of yours. You're so much more than just a psychic. I'll have to create a new name for you."

"Good evening dear guests," Chance shared in the salutations, "It's a pleasure to meet you. Rhea, you're always full of compliments. You mustn't flatter me too much in front of these lovely people. I don't deserve it." Chance blushed as she made her introduction—she was obviously embarrassed by Rhea's comment.

Although Chance seemed younger than Rhea by a few years, she also seemed equally mature and courteous. Chance had a very distinctive dress sense. She looked as if she had thrown on every item in her wardrobe, creating a peculiar layered look. Somehow, she pulled it off beautifully.

Rhea moved on to the next person sitting opposite of Chance.

"This is Dameer, who is our very own in house psychologist, and his main areas of interest are dreams and hypnosis."

"Pleased to meet you all," Dameer highlighted, "I'm afraid I'd also like to have an alternative title, Rhea, since mine sounds quite wacky and abstract!"

He winked at Rhea as she walked past him.

"I promise I won't hypnotize any of you into becoming farm animals," Dameer went on, "My work will surprise you. It is unlike any other experience you have stumbled upon."

Dameer was older than both Rhea and Chance. Life's lessons were visible on the deep lines around his eyes and forehead. He had an infectious smile that introduced the guests to his humorous nature.

"Yes you're right Dameer, but let's not reveal too much to our new friends," said Rhea, "We wouldn't want to ruin all the fun, now would we?"

"And this is Latifah, our very own masseuse." Rhea continued as she moved behind the lady sitting next to Dameer.

Latifah's bright green eyes contrasted beautifully against her olive colored skin. She had long black her, which hung, loosely against her back.

"She's been known to make grown men cry with the healing powers of her wonderful hands," added Rhea.

"Good evening," said Latifah, "Rhea's right. A man did cry, but perhaps because I almost broke his spine!"

The staff all laughed, leaving the guests once again unsure about the nature of her statement. Was it a joke? The four guests continued to smile politely and curiously listened as Rhea introduced the last person.

Putting her arm on his shoulders, she said, "Of course, last but not least, this is Adam. He's our resident chef."

"Nice meeting you all," Expressed Adam, "I hope to tantalize your taste buds to the best of my ability. The foods you'll be having won't only be delicious, but they will also be made with ingredients of the utmost healing power. Just like every other activity here at the Karma Hotel, each meal will be carefully personalized to meet your individual needs."

"In other words, you'll be put on a diet of brussel sprouts and cabbage soup!" Dameer once again broke the seriousness of his colleagues' statement with a joke.

Just as their laughter was dying down, Alexander spotted a beautiful white Persian cat jumping on one of the chairs. He loved cats but was never allowed to have one as a child because his mother was allergic to them.

"Look at this little beauty!"

Everyone turned their attention to the graceful and majestic creature. Rhea walked towards the cat and it immediately jumped in to her arms.

"I was wrong. We haven't finished with the introductions. Meet Magic. He is one of the most important elements of our establishment, and as his name indicates, he is truly a special and mystical creature."

Adriana, Jennifer and Alexander walked over to pet the cat. Magic looked content in Rhea's arms, and his purr could be heard across the room. It was such a calm and passive cat, clearly enjoying the company and attention of everyone. He had a beautiful silver collar around his neck, with what appeared to be a small bell attached to it. *If only it was just a bell! I'm sure*

Rhea would be more than displeased at hearing Magic's source of power as being described by just a round metal object, capable of mostly causing irritation. Nevertheless, for now, my wanderlust, we shall refer to it as a bell.

The new diner members took turns holding Magic; he stayed nestled comfortably in their arms and continued to purr. It was as if Magic were also welcoming the visitors, in his own way.

"I've never seen such a gorgeous looking cat, not to mention how happy he is to be held by total strangers!"

Adriana had had two cats of her own in the past. They were so different from Magic—not friendly at all—and they always slept under her bed and would go into hiding at the first sight of visitors.

Daniel remained seated at the opposite end of the table. He did not care too much for animals, let alone cats. He thought them to be too detached and arrogant. 'Weren't there enough people like that in the world?' He pondered: why someone would choose to have a cat as a pet was a mystery to Daniel. 'They walk around the house as if they own the place, and they don't acknowledge you much unless they are hungry and otherwise spend all day napping. Fun! Why not get a picture of a cat and hang it on the wall? Think how much money people would save on cat food'.

Suddenly, Magic jumped out of Jennifer's arms and walked slowly across the dinning table towards Daniel. The cat's behavior was truly amazing. Everyone watched as he made his way towards the last guest. It seemed as if he wanted to greet Daniel as well, so that he would not feel left out. It was almost as if he had read Daniel's thoughts and wanted to prove him wrong. Magic stopped in front of Daniel, laid down on his back and began rolling back and forth. He started to lightly paw at Daniel's hand, purring louder than before. Daniel still remained indifferent.

"I'm sorry, but I've never really liked cats," he said, finally feeling the need to explain his lack of enthusiasm towards the animal. From his expressions, it was obvious how uncomfortable he felt.

"Don't worry Daniel, Magic will soon take care of that. However, I will set the stage for him by warning all of you—he is not just any ordinary cat."

Rhea smiled with utmost confidence. She lowered her voice into a whisper and then said, "so please don't refer to him as that or else you will upset him."

Magic slowly returned to all fours, but he still remained in front of Daniel. All of a sudden, he shook his head furiously from side to side. The bell around his collar started to chime. It was a very different sound, so pleasant, like a gentle massage of the ears, like a familiar tune you knew as a child. Daniel blinked a few times, and the light in the room seemed to be getting dimmer.

When he finally opened his eyes, he immediately realized that he was no longer at the Karma Hotel. None of his new friends or the people he had just met were anywhere in sight. Still, he did not feel lost, nervous or scared. On the contrary, this was the most familiar and happy scene he could have ever returned to. He had somehow been teleported to his grandmother's house. He could see her standing in the kitchen, cooking his favorite meal: rice with meatballs and potatoes in a tomato sauce. The aroma of her cooking teased his senses, bringing back so many happy memories.

At once, Daniel was filled with much appreciation and love for her. He remembered how she was the only one who believed him about the voices. She would grab him into such a firm embrace, as if to hug all the pain and confusion away. She even said that she had 'friends' of her own that no one else could see. Later, he found out it was because of those 'friends' that his grandfather could finally take no more, and left him.

For once in his life he was thankful about these strange mental abilities he had. The whole scene with that cat at the dining room of the Karma Hotel had left him a little anxious. Therefore he must have chosen to block everyone out in order to return to a more calm and loving atmosphere, or so he rationalized his sudden change of perspective.

"I'm sorry Daniel, but I can't let you take credit for this one."

Startled, Daniel looked around to see which one of the voices was speaking. In front of him, he saw Magic lounging on his grandmother's favorite chair. Was the cat talking to him?! What was he doing here anyway?! Now Daniel was sure he had lost it!

Again, Magic had read his mind, and the cat spoke back to him, telepathically.

"Yes, it's me who said those words and brought you here. What a wonderful home. You loved it here as a child, right? Too bad you never told your grandmother how much you loved her or showed her your appreciation for soothing your soul on those blue days," whispered Magic.

It took a few seconds for Daniel to digest this whole scene, to fully take in the impact of this experience.

When he finally felt his heartbeat return to normal, he said, "You can talk, Magic?! This is crazy, man! Wait 'til I tell Dr. Hartly about this. He'll lock me up for sure!"

"Yes I can talk, among other things. I felt your uneasiness and chose you as my first volunteer to demonstrate my position in the Karma Hotel. Do you know why I opted to return you to your grandmother's house?"

"Well, other than the fact that you've totally freaked me out and almost made my heart stop, no, I'm not really sure. But I guess an explanation is on its way, right?"

The whole time neither Daniel nor Magic spoke aloud—they communicated through their thoughts.

"Of course I'll explain—if you need an explanation. We've come back here for me to offer you the opportunity to express your gratitude to your grandmother, to let her know how much she helped you when you needed it. Isn't it something you've always wanted to do? Didn't she pass away before you could?" Magic remained seated on the chair as he explained.

"So, does she know we're here? Will she recognize me?" Daniel was both curious and confused about what was going on.

"She will, but don't think too much about the logistics of our brief journey. Let your mind follow your heart. Walk up to her and leave the rest up to your emotions. Let them be your guide."

Daniel started walking towards the kitchen. He felt his heart race once again. Was he going to talk to a ghost? Had he died himself? Was this the episode of extreme distortion between reality and fantasy that Dr Hartley always warned him about? 'Shut up Daniel, shut up!! Keep walking! Do as the cat says!' He chuckled at the absurdity of his situation.

Daniel's Grandmother was happily stirring the meatball sauce, humming one of her favorite love songs, reminiscing about the times she and Daniel's grandfather danced in the kitchen while she cooked their favorite dishes. She turned around, as if she suddenly sensed Daniel's presence behind her.

"Daniel! My sweet angel, how I've missed you so! I knew you were coming to visit your crazy grandmother today so I prepared your favorite meal."

She threw her arms around her grandson and gave him one of those bone-breaking hugs. *Don't they feel so much better than weak hugs? What good is an embrace if it isn't empowered by all your heart and soul?*

"Grandma, you're not crazy; I've missed you too. Mmmmmmmmmm, the food smells so good!"

"Let me look at my little boy. Doesn't he look handsome and all grown up. How's medical school my child? Are you a doctor yet? I've been having this ache in the lower part of my back. Maybe you could …"

Daniel responded quickly, interrupting her before she finished her sentence. "No grandma, I'm not a doctor yet, maybe in my next life!" He said jokingly. "But I need to talk to you about something," he went on, "and I don't know how long I can stay so let me get right to the point …"

Daniel's Grandmother suddenly looked worried, took off her apron and sat down on one of the chairs around her kitchen table.

"I'm ok Grandma. I just wanted to see you again, even if it's for a few minutes. I want to thank you for always being there for me—especially when I was growing up. During those days, you always made me feel normal amongst people who tried to say I was different and weird. Maybe when I was a kid I was stupid and did not really show you all this stuff I'm telling you now, but you always meant so much to me …"

Daniel felt so liberated by letting his emotions govern him.

"… Especially your hugs followed by your killer meat ball sauce and rice, what else could a guy ask for?"

Daniel got up from his chair and hugged his grandmother as tightly as he could.

"My sweet little Daniel, maybe you never said these words to me but your cute sneaky smiles always confirmed your love towards me. Anyhow, thank you for coming to see me," She wiped her tears with a napkin she had hidden under her left sleeve, "You'll never be alone my angel; I'll always be near, watching and praying for you."

"Thanks Grandma, I love you."

Daniel did not want to let her go. ***Her scent cradled his soul so gently. Why is it that grand mothers smell so good? Along with wisdom and life experience, it must be a characteristic of old age.***

The next thing he heard was the chime of the bells from Magic's collar. Daniel opened his eyes. He was still being held, but not by his grandmother. It was Rhea embracing him. He was back in the dining room of the Karma Hotel and everything looked exactly as he had remembered. Everyone was in the same position, talking away casually about this and that, petting Magic and getting to know each other.

Daniel pulled away from Rhea's arms slowly and looked at her with bewildered eyes.

"Don't worry Daniel, this is our little secret, no one knows. You were chosen by Magic to have the first experience. The others will have their turn," She winked at him as she walked away.

Daniel remained silent and somewhat overwhelmed by the whole experience. He wanted to call his mother right away to tell her that he had seen grandmother and that she looked beautiful and healthy, engaging in her daily activities. But she'd probably call Dr. Hartley right away. He dismissed the idea quickly.

Everyone remained in the dining room for a while longer, ate some light snacks and engaged in small talk with the people working there. It was already close to midnight when Rhea said good night to the guests.

"I wish we could stay longer with each other; this has been so delightful," Rhea accentuated, "However it is late and we have an eventful three days ahead of us, starting tomorrow." She stroked Magic as she spoke. "So have a good evening and may you all sleep tight. Sweet dreams, my friends."

Everyone embraced as they said their goodnights. How quickly they had bonded, gotten to know each other. They were like old friends, not at all like people who had just met.

"But just before you sleep," Rhea continued, "I need you to start your first exercise. There is a notebook in the drawer of your bedside table."

Rhea looked more serious and authoritative than before as she began instructing them.

"Take the notebook out, along with the pen provided for you, and start to recount the way in which you were contacted by us. Sort of like the summary of events that led you to the Karma hotel."

Adriana liked the idea. She had been itching to tell her friends and family members about the Karma Hotel but, just as our other guests, was strictly instructed not to in her invitation. This was the perfect chance for her to recount her story. However, Adriana's enthusiasm was soon replaced by curiosity regarding the purpose of the assignment.

"Excuse my ignorance Rhea, but could you tell us why you would need to be told about those events when it was you who arranged this meeting?" Adriana tried to sound as tactful as possible.

"That's a very good question my dear," said Rhea, always so positive and nurturing, "not at all an ignorant one."

"You see, you were all contacted in different ways, some of you more than a few times. Therefore it would be interesting for us to know which method proved to be most successful and why. It would provide more insight regarding the way in which you perceived our invitation and why you accepted it."

Her next comment surprised all of the guests.

"You see my special visitors—we contact many people from all around the world, through different methods. Some choose to acknowledge our invitation, while others simply ignore it and continue living in darkness.

"Maybe it's because they are afraid of the truth, or maybe it's because the idea of shedding light onto their problem or issues is more painful than enduring it. Maybe people are afraid of change or of the unknown and so they choose to live their life in the status quo."

Alexander could not believe that there were individuals out there who would miss such a mystical opportunity.

Dameer stood up to add to Rhea's points:

"These matters put forth by Rhea don't just relate to acceptance of the invitation—they also apply to anyone who is in an unfortunate situation and is not experiencing a fulfilled spiritual existence. Sadly, no matter who tries to help such individuals—advise them or enlighten them—they remain resistant to crucial change."

Dameer looked down as he spoke, as if his script were written on the table.

"Everyone is unique in his or her own way," He continued, "as are the choices we make regarding our perceived happiness. So your input on why and how you accepted the invitation will give us all a glimpse into who you are."

Rhea chose her next words delicately.

"Please note we must also respect the choices of those who don't reply to our calling. That's their prerogative and we are not in the business of judging people. We are here to help the individuals who are ready, in any way we can. Your first entry in the journals will give us more insight regarding what sets you apart from those people who choose to ignore our invitations."

Alexander, Jennifer, Daniel and Adriana seemed comfortable, and more importantly, convinced by the explanation put forth. They said good night to the members of the Hotel and made their way across the lobby towards the elevator.

"I wonder if we'll be allowed to read each other's journal entries," shared Jennifer, "I'd love to know how you guys got invited."

From the look on Daniel's face, Jennifer realized he would defiantly not let her read his.

"Journals are private things, Jennifer. Didn't you ever keep one when you were younger?" Alexander asked, trying to ease the tension as usual.

"I used to have one, but my mom read it and I got into a lot of trouble. So I threw it away and never kept one again."

Adriana suddenly got a flashback of her mother yelling at her after reading her diary. Her mother had found out about her kissing Michael, her first boy-friend, at the innocent age of 14.

"Well, maybe we can all get together, to have a reunion or something in a couple of years and talk about it then. That is if we haven't been locked up in a mental institute somewhere for talking about some of the things that go on here."

Daniel was thinking about his meeting with his grandmother, about Magic's abilities and what a strange character Rhea was. He thought she might be a witch but he decided not to share that with the rest of the group.

"Oh Daniel, let it go! Just try and enjoy this, will you?"

Alexander was not going to let the depressed one dampen his spirits. He was determined to make the most of this experience. So was Daniel—but unfortunately his 'unwelcome visitors,' sarcasm and skepticism, always got the upper hand. It was time to kick both of the rude intruders out, and invite inquisitiveness and imagination over, just as his guest companions had.

ℰᏇᏇᏇℰᏇᏇ

The Beginning of the Magic

"To see the world in a grain of sand,
and a heaven in a wild flower,
hold infinity in the palm of your hand,
and eternity in an hour."

—William Blake (*Auguries of Innocence*)

Journal Entries

ഇ‌ാര‌ോഇ‌ാര‌ോഇ‌ാര‌ോഇ‌ാര‌ോ

Jennifer

About a month ago, I was doing some research in the library. I had an essay to write for one of my psychology classes regarding sexual orientation. My lecturer had been specific in what he required. Other than a clear explanation of the different preferences, possible causes and social consequences, he asked us to include a relevant case study. So I had spent most of the afternoon searching for a recent account of someone struggling with, or coming to terms with, his or her attraction towards the same gender.

Not being very successful with my search, I started to get anxious and bored, so I went to look at some of the travel books located at the other end of the library to give my mind a break. Suddenly, I came across a book called *Coming Out of the Closet and Into the Light*. It must have been misplaced, because it was in the wrong section. Nevertheless, I opened it and it had exactly what I was looking for; a case study about a middle-aged woman struggling with her sexuality. It was on the last page of the article that I found your invitation.

Of course, I didn't know the paper was an invitation at the time. It seemed to be old, rather tarnished and worn out. As usual, my curiosity got the best of me, and I started reading it. What shocked me was that it was addressed to me! My full name was written on top. The rest of the information described what I was going through and my desire to learn more about my connection to Austria. I looked over my shoulder to see if anyone was watching me, if this was a practical joke or if one of my friends was hiding behind the bookshelf, giggling. After all, most of my family members and friends were aware of my unexplainable curiosity and were quite sick of hearing about it! There was no one there. So I closed the book, checked it out of the library and took both the invitation and the book home to read them again privately.

At first I was in shock and disbelief. I didn't know what to make of it. The note asked me to write to an address if I was interested in finding out more about the promises the invitation made, and so I did. I thought it was harmless enough. I gave my college address rather than my private one for some reason. But the tone of the note was so comforting and safe. I know that might sound crazy, but that's how I felt. So I went with my instinct and wrote back. I had spent so long pondering over why I felt attached to Austria. I've only been there once, but have always had the urge to return. None of the books or tapes on past lives that I bought explained my experiences adequately. They just left me more confused and frustrated than I started out! But, somehow, this time I felt that my search would not end in vein, and even if it did, I was willing to try anything to uncover the truth.

As instructed by the invitation, I didn't tell anyone. That was hell for me! I was dying to share the possibility of discovering my odd connection to Austria with my best friend. But I abided by the rules and remained silent. The hardest part was leaving my friends to come here. They kept asking me where I was going and why. I told them I had an uncle who lived up north and I was going to see him and my long lost cousins. I don't know if they bought it or not, but I guess that doesn't matter now that I'm here. I feel so lucky to have been chosen. Thank you very much!

ᏕᏯᏠᏰᏯᏠᏕᏯᏠᏰᏯᏠᏕᏯᏠᏰᏯᏠ

Alexander

What a beautiful journey this has been, to such a wonderful place. I spent many nights thinking about coming here, and the Karma Hotel has far exceeded my expectations. Where do I start? I guess the beginning would be appropriate, right? Well, it was about a month ago when I received your message. My fatigue and periods of exhaustion were at their peak, keeping me in bed for hours. I work at a homeless shelter, and my boss was getting more than irritated with my absenteeism.

I tried to explain that I'm not lazy or slacking off, but how could I offer a valid excuse to him when my understanding of my condition is so sketchy? After going to various types of doctors and healers, I decided to try something new. After all, none of them had offered me any helpful explanations. Sure they all had their own special theories, but that confused me even further, because all their explanations differed. It's not their fault really. Doctors are only human. They are beautiful and special people who devote their lives to trying to help others, but they shouldn't be expected to know everything.

I had been at the mall that afternoon, buying a present for my brother. When I returned to my car, I found a leaflet on my windshield. It was from a psychic called Alba who claimed to be exceptional in her field. So when I got home, I called her, made an appointment, and then went to see her the following day.

She was waiting for me at the door as I pulled up into her driveway. She looked so familiar, I felt like we had met before, but maybe that's what all her clients tell her. We sat down at her round dining table and chatted a while before beginning my reading. I guess she is a psychic and a clairvoyant. The reason I say this is because half way through reading my tarot cards, she started talking out loud to someone. Someone invisible, a spirit perhaps, I never really asked her. You see we were alone in that room, but she was talking to this third entity as if it were sitting with us.

The spirit's voice came through very strong, Alba said. It was asking to speak to me through her. Through the spirit, Alba described my feelings and condition perfectly, even better than I ever could. Then it told her to tell me that everything would be ok, that I could be cured soon.

The spirit gave her an address for me to respond to if I was interested in finding out more. I quickly jotted down the information and waited for more from her. Well, there was no more, the session ended after that. Alba looked worn out and she said she was unable to continue. The spirit's presence had been so strong that the whole experience had drained her. I thanked her for what she had done and left.

I wrote to the address right after I got home. I was so excited and interested to know more, so excited that I've been very restless for the last few weeks. I'm not sure how you got to me through Alba, but I suppose it's all part of the mystical essence of the Karma Hotel. I know it's still premature to make any kind of predictions about my experience, but I feel so much better already, even before we have begun! Thank you Rhea, Dameer, Chance, Latifah, Adam and of course Magic!

ဢာ) G⅜ဢာ)G⅜ဢာ)G⅜ဢာ)G⅜

Daniel

I'm not very good at writing stuff like this, nor am I sure I remember the exact details of that night, but I will try my best. I'm sorry if it sounds stupid.

I was at home about a month ago. It was a very warm night so I decided to have a beer. I sat in front of the TV, watched one stupid sitcom after another, and drank. I started off with only one bottle of beer, but it soon became two, then three, four and five. I lost count after the eighth one. I'm not sure why but I got angrier with every sip I took.

Everything started to frustrate me: the voice of the actors, the feel of the sofa I was sitting on, the flowers on the wallpaper, even the color of the curtains. It was as if the environment had turned into my imaginary enemy. I hated everything about it, and it hated me in return. I don't think anyone else was home at first. My mom came home half way through my "tantrum" as she calls it.

She had seen me act that way before and usually ignored it until I came back to my senses. The best way to shake off these crazy feelings is just to sleep it off. That seems to do the trick for me, sometimes. But that night, the thought of trying to fall asleep made me even more anxious. I just couldn't relax. So I went into the garage, grabbed the baseball bat, and decided to destroy anything that frustrated me in the living room. I started with the TV, moved on to the windows, the pictures on the walls, then the table and just about any other object in my way.

Anyway, my mom came home eventually. She watched me for a while, crying hysterically. Finally, she realized that this episode couldn't be ignored. She called the police, and to make a long story short, I ended up at the local police station, in one of their cells. To be honest with you, I was so comfortable there. I felt so safe, I don't know from whom, maybe from myself. The whole situation sobered me up really quick. I felt so guilty for the way I had acted and for making my mom's life a living hell.

I knew I had to change. I couldn't go on living like that, but I swear this wasn't the first time I tried to make it all go away. Things would be fine for a while, and then Boom! I'd have another relapse into that miserable guy who ended up in jail. So I started making all sorts of promises to myself, like to try to let others like my mom and Dr Hartley help me, to not be so negative and bitter all the time and to basically shape up.

I fell asleep while having those thoughts. It was there that I had one of the most vivid dreams of my life. It was so clear and detailed, as if I were watching TV or something. A beautiful woman came to talk to me in the cell. She looked kind of like Rhea now that I think about it. She walked in, embraced me and told me that everything would be ok. She knew all about my condition, even about the voices and people only I could see. I was shocked! No one knew about them, not even Dr Hartley. She said that she could try to help me, gave me an address for me to write to if I was interested, embraced me again and walked out.

I must have awakened just as the dream ended because the details were still so fresh in my mind. I called out to one of the guards and asked him to jot down the address for me.

When I got home later that day, I wrote to the people she'd told me about, expressing my interest. I had nothing to lose, even if it was some crazy dream. That night I decided to make a change, so I was willing to try anything. I didn't tell anyone anything as you guys instructed. I told my mom I was going to visit an old high school friend, and she seemed to buy the story.

I'm sorry if I seem like an asshole sometimes. I don't know why I have this much anger and bitterness in me. I guess maybe you guys will be able to help me with that, but please understand that deep down inside I'm really a good guy. I'm just tired of being tortured mentally.

ଛଉଚ୍ଚଛଉଚ୍ଚଛଉଚ୍ଚଛଉଚ୍ଚ

Adriana

(The Way in Which I was Invited to The Karma Hotel)

I've been staring at the title above for the past five minutes, trying to get my thoughts together about what to write. Well, maybe I know what to write but I'm not sure how to clearly express my feelings about the events of that day. It was a combination of shock, happiness, excitement, and above all, hope.

I had spent the previous evening with Stephen. We had gone to dinner and then watched a beautiful French movie. I can't recall the name right now because the events that preceded it overshadowed the details of the movie, including the name. We went to my house, as we usually do. I sometimes joke about being tired of spending time in my apartment. I ask him sometimes if we can go to his house for a change and maybe ask his wife to make us a meal. Of course he has always been less than amused, ignored my comment and gave me a sneaky side stare.

What can I say? He is the love of my life, perfect in every way, except for one small minor detail; he's been married for the past 11 years, has 3 children and will not discuss divorcing her. Not that I ever initiate a conversation on the subject, but on those occasions when the matter has crept its way into our midnight discussions, he's made his position quite clear. Divorce is not an option. See, the irony of it all is that I love him for the same reason I hate him. I love him for being such a caring soul who would rather die than hurt anyone, yet this selfless being is killing me slowly by refusing to end a loveless marriage to avoid hurting his wife and kids.

Ok, I've lost focus now. Where was I? Yes, back to my apartment. We had a beautiful evening, ate ice cream on the couch while watching TV, made mad passionate love in front of the fireplace and then held each other all night. I'm sure Stephen and I even have the same dreams. We are so connected that even the night or a different state of consciousness, such as sleep, couldn't separate us. He finishes my sentences, surprises me with gifts I've always dreamed of since childhood, and says words to me that would put Shakespeare, Gibran and Rumi to shame. God, I love this man. Why couldn't I have met him 12 years ago?

We woke up the next morning, still wrapped in each other's arms. I felt a sense of panic engulfing me. I knew he had to leave early and wasn't sure when I'd see him again. So I started a fight. Maybe it was my way of prolonging his stay; maybe it was a desperate cry for how much I needed him. Or maybe it was that I finally had had enough of sharing him. I started to cry, and we fought for a while; and he eventually left with no real resolution to our conflict.

I was heart broken, yet again. I went to the café down the street from my apartment and ordered a cappuccino. The waiter noticed I had been crying and was sitting alone. After watching me for awhile, the waiter approached my table. He asked if I was ok or if I wanted another coffee, on the house. I thanked him politely, feeling so touched by this stranger's act of kindness.

He asked if he could sit down for a moment. I said yes, not thinking twice about the invitation, knowing he worked there. I didn't remember seeing him before, however, so I thought he must be a new employee. He sat down and started talking about his own problems. He described being in a relationship exactly like the one I was caught up in! The same situation, similar details, and problems that I faced. I was shocked, but in a way comforted with the idea that I wasn't alone in what I was feeling. I didn't reveal any details about my life—just listened to the stranger.

He then told me that regardless of what I was going through, he knew of someone who might be able to help. The same person or people had helped him. He wouldn't give me any more details about 'who' they were, only an address of where to contact them if I was interested. The man said if I took the initiative to write to these people, they would get back to me within a few days.

I took the address, thanked him, paid the bill and went home. I opened the door of my apartment to find the whole house filled with bouquets of roses. That's the kind of man Stephen is. He always makes me feel so special, so lucky for knowing him, even during an argument. I kicked Sadness out of my house and invited Hope back in. I immediately wrote to the address that the waiter had given me and eagerly awaited a reply.

Your response arrived four days later. I got an official invitation and was told not to discuss the details of my trip with anyone. I was dying to tell my sister about the events of the last few days. She would have said that the waiter was probably an angel sent to me in my time of need, and maybe she would be right. The next day I went to the same café and asked for the waiter who had eased my restless soul. The other employees gave me a puzzled look and said they didn't have anyone working there by that description.

So here I am. I'm not sure who the waiter was or why he chose me, but I'm very eager to start this journey of enlightenment. I have not been able to find any earthly reason as to why I love Stephen so much or why I continue to punish myself by staying with him. Maybe we are connected in some bigger way that only you can help me see. Thank you for coming to me at a time when I so desperately need some answers.

ಬಡಚ್ಚಡಚ್ಚಡಚ್ಚಡಚ

Color Magic

"Mere color, unspoiled by meaning, and unallied with definite form, can speak to the soul in a thousand different ways."

—Oscar Wilde (*The Critic as Artist*)

The next morning, Alexander, Adriana, Jennifer and Daniel were permitted to rest peacefully. They had a busy schedule ahead of them for the next three days, but sleep and relaxation were an implicit part of the treatment and so guests were always encouraged to rest as much as they pleased. Their rooms were designed in such a way as to offer optimum comfort and relaxation, down to the last detail. Even though each room was decorated differently, the rooms were identical in the way that comfort and tranquility were the main themes employed when considering design, colors and use of space.

As each new group of guests arrived, the rooms were slightly altered to meet each individual's different needs. *If you remember, dear reader, the main feature of Alexander's room was the huge comfortable bed the hotel had ordered especially for him. The other rooms had equally comfortable beds, but for some reason, his was a little more special.*

The staff was aware of Alexander's bouts of exhaustion and believed relaxation would be an essential part of his healing. The rest of the room was beautifully decorated with different shades of green: apple, forest, grass and lime to name a few. Rhea was knowledgeable about the practices of ancient Chinese and Indian healers who used different colors as an intrinsic part of curing those in need. She knew that each color has a unique vibration and power. Green was used for Alexander, due to its calming and restful vibration, along with white, which was used in all the rooms as a base color. White has long been used for psychic matters, to dispel evil spirits and for new beginnings.

Along with color, aromatherapy was also used due to its many beneficial properties. Electrical vaporizers containing water and a few drops of the particular essential oil that best suited each guest, were placed in different areas of the room. In Alexander's case, Latifah, the Hotel's expert in the field of aromatherapy, had recommended the pure essential oil of tangerine peels because of its ability to calm and relax.

Alexander opened his eyes and looked around his room. He resisted waking up for a moment, wanting to slip back into the heavenly slumber that had kidnapped him all night. It took him a few seconds to realize where he was. He played the events of the day before in his mind, as if he were watching one of his favorite movies.

His heart and soul filled with love as he thought about Rhea and the other members of the hotel. He couldn't wait to see them again, to get started with the different activities planned for them. He jumped out of bed thinking aloud, 'when was the last time I felt so happy about waking up? So enthusiastic and energetic about starting my day?' *Do you remember when the last time was that you woke up engulfed with such vitality? Perhaps it's been too long my friend.*

Alexander headed straight for the shower, stopping only briefly at the window to take in the magnificent view of the surrounding mountains. He did not want to be late, so he continued towards the bathroom.

Jennifer had set her alarm for ten o'clock. She knew Rhea had not specified what time they should meet, but she was already too excited to sleep and decided that she did not need more than eight hours to feel revitalized. The soft beeping sound slowly beckoned her back to consciousness. She immediately opened her eyes, and scanned the beautiful and hospitable room, which was brilliantly decorated in different shades of brown and yellow. Could Rhea have known that autumn was her favorite time of the year? Maybe this was Chance's input through her psychic powers. Her room seemed like a scene from a beautiful park on a sunny fall afternoon. She could not have felt more at home.

Rhea and Chance had chosen those colors specifically for Jennifer. Yellow is meant to stimulate the mind and represent knowledge and reflection, while brown acts as a protective shield for adventurous minds and denotes an active intellect and attraction to nature.

The scent of the oils burning on the electrical vaporizers had completely invaded and occupied the room. She tried to figure out the top note of the scent but found it difficult to distinguish its fragrance. She later asked Latifah, who told Jennifer she had used a combination of jasmine, patchouli, and sandalwood. The effect was like having massive bouquets of different kinds of flowers around her.

Jennifer wasn't sure what the effects of these particular oils were, but she knew she felt deeply relaxed and indescribably balanced. She found it hard to explain, but it was as if her curiosity about so many things regarding her life that constantly haunted her had suddenly ceased to exist. She felt comfortable with who she was and where she was going in life. For the first time, the past didn't preoccupy herself; the present and the future seemed more interesting. It was time to find out what both held for her in the next few days. She started getting ready so she could meet the others in the lobby.

Tossing and turning all night as the hours passed, Daniel had not slept very well. At the same time, however, he did not feel exhausted when morning arrived nor did he feel the same anger as at home upon waking up. Maybe that was because he did not want to fall asleep. Maybe, for the first time in a very long time, he wanted to stay awake, entertaining life rather than closing himself off to it.

Sleep had always been a way for Daniel to shut himself out of this terrible world, to drown all the voices, both real and imaginary. Sleep was an escape to a safer place where experiences were not 'real'. If ever he was uncomfortable with the images in dreams, he would simply wake himself up. What a great way to flee an undesirable situation. He liked that sense of control as he seemed not to have it in waking hours.

Since yesterday, Daniel's urge to escape, to run away from the world had subsided. He used his first night at the hotel as a way to think about his life, what he had been through and his relationship with his mother. He knew he had made her life miserable for too long.

He wasn't going to let her continue living without knowing how much he loved and appreciated her. He needed to tell her how sorry he was. He thought about his journey with Magic. If it wasn't for that crazy cat, he may have never had the opportunity to speak to his grandmother again. He decided he would not let history repeat itself; he would enjoy and appreciate his mother's presence as long as she lived.

Why do we need such monumental events like a death to appreciate loved ones? Can we not give to those precious to us when they are but a few steps away? Why do we suddenly remember our love for them when they are six feet under ground?

Daniel drank from all the different types of juices that Adam had left for him. He looked around his room, admiring the way it was decked out. Such a contrast to his gloomy, dark and morbid room at home, he thought. The walls were a brilliant white ablaze with radiance. Were those sparkles he saw on the curtain or was that the light creating that effect? Along with white, different shades of purple and blue were scattered across the room.

He looked at the beautiful purple couch he had laid on all night. It was so plush and soft. He thought about the way the couch grabbed him, almost embraced him, rocking him to sleep.

Rhea had specifically chosen those colors in an attempt to break through Daniel's defenses. After all, blue was the color of the spirit and represented healing, idealism and occult protection; and purple is for spiritual growth, strengthening our link with the universe and higher planes. Daniel seemed to be in great need of all those things.

Daniel did not like the aroma being released form those electric vaporizers however. The scent reminded him of medication and the vitamins he was forced to take as a child. But if he ignored his cynicism and negativity for only a few seconds, he could detect the beautiful scent of rose as the main fragrance penetrating the atmosphere.

Latifah had told Rhea about the eleventh century Islamic philosopher, Avicenna, who distilled roses to help his patients suffering from deep rooted feelings such as grief, anger and various forms of mood disorders. It had worked with previous guests so they decided to use rose along with some other plants. Daniel was right about the pungent scent of Frankincense, Lemongrass and Vetiver, which were mixed in to maximize the psychological benefits of the oils.

Just as Daniel was contemplating whether or not to turn off the vaporizer, he heard a knock on the door. Had he not hung the "Do not disturb" sign? Had he ordered room service? He stood facing the door and said, "Who is it? Can I help you?"

"Hey Daniel, it's me, Alexander. I was just on my way to the lobby and thought I'd stop to see if you were ready. We could walk down together."

Daniel opened the door and invited Alexander in.

"Wow ... I didn't know all the rooms were so different! Look at that couch!" Alexander's face lit up like a kid in a candy store.

"It feels even better than it looks. Give it a try. Throw yourself on it. It's so comfortable."

Daniel watched Alexander as he ran towards the couch. He took a few steps back and then threw himself on it like a young boy would.

"Ohhhh maaaaaaaan, this is almost as nice as my bed! Oh Daniel, you have to try my bed; it's the most comfortable thing I've ever slept on!"

"Hey, I believe you. This place is amazing—they have the best of everything. Try some of that apple juice in my mini bar."

Daniel headed for the bathroom while Alexander finished two small bottles of the apple juice.

"I'm going to tell Adam you're finishing my juice!" Daniel teased.

"I'll have to ask him why I didn't get any of this stuff! You're right, it's delicious," replied Alexander, "Go ahead and finish getting ready. I'll wait for you here."

"Ok, I won't be long. You think the girls are ready yet?"

"I don't think so. Maybe Jennifer, but not Adriana. I'll call her to let her know we're almost ready."

Alexander did not want Adriana to miss any part of the process.

The ring of the phone awakened Adriana. She desperately wanted to finish the dream she was having, so she tried hard to ignore it. She imagined a phone, and kept picking it up in her dream, but the ringing didn't stop. At last she was forced to open her eyes, to abandon the scene wherein she and Stephen were having a very serious and real discussion about their future. Her dream was so coherent and clear, no interpretations needed—no hidden signs or symbols; just clear-cut conversation about their love for each other. Trying to hide her irritation, and sleepy voice, she cleared her throat before answering.

"I knew you were still asleep, you little angel!"

Alexander's sweet voice was distinguishable; even though it was the first time she had heard him on the phone.

"Good morning Alexander. Were you up at the crack of dawn with the roosters?" Adriana could not help throwing that comment in.

Alexander was just a little too cheerful for that time of the day, she thought, and 'What time was it anyway?' Adriana looked at her watch and realized it was not that early after all. She hated being late, and worse yet, making others wait for her.

"Oh, I'm so sorry Alexander. Am I late?" Adriana panicked for a second.

"No, not at all" Alexander replied, "Don't worry about it. We're still not ready. Take your time. We'll meet you in the lobby in about 30 minutes. How's that Adrianna?"

"That sounds great; I'll be there. Have you spoken to the others?"

"Yes, I'm with Daniel now, and I'm going to call Jennifer after I hang up with you. Adriana, how's your room?"

"It's incredible Alexander, indescribable maybe, but I'll do my best to tell you all about it when I see you. Now let me get ready!"

"Ok, ok. Daniel says good morning. See you in the lobby!" And with that they hung up.

Adriana pondered Alexander's question regarding her room. She looked around taking in every little detail that made up this mini-heaven created just for her. How did they know she absolutely loved the color red? Was it a coincidence that her curtains were made of the exact material she had seen in a magazine a month ago?

She had instantly fallen in love with the design, colors and fabric. She had promised herself to put some time aside for buying and hanging those curtains in her bedroom, and suddenly, here they were. She thought, if Cupid had a bedroom, it would look the same as her room, so romantic, warm and cozy. The shades of these two colors ranged from baby pink to rose to blood red to crimson and some burgundy. Her comforter cover looked as if someone had splashed red wine on it. Then, as a way to add another dimension, there were scattered rose petals all over. The entire room glistened with vivacity.

Rhea had chosen these colors due to their vibrations and association with the life force, vitality and determination. Red, being one of the most powerful colors, is meant to empower and attract good luck. Pink was woven into Adriana's color therapy as an element of harmony, happiness and of course love. Its vibrations to balance the mind and the heart had already started to affect her. Or was that the beautiful essential oils at work? Adriana could not get enough of them. She kept walking up to the tables where the vaporizers were placed to inhale the wonderful fragrances being released into the air.

Adriana got regular aromatherapy massages, and so she could recognize the exquisite scents of Ylang Ylang and Lavender. She knew both were excellent for anxiety and insomnia. She couldn't identify the other hints of aroma. Latifah had also mixed in Bergamot, Patchouli and Peppermint, which have a calming effect but are also known for their ability to ground our energy, to help us think more clearly and may sometimes work as aphrodisiacs. No wonder Adriana had been dreaming about Stephen all night. She suddenly realized she had only 15 minutes left before she was due to meet with the others. She rushed into the bathroom and started getting ready.

ℬ⊃ℭℛℬ⊃ℭℛℬ⊃ℭℛℬ⊃ℭℛ

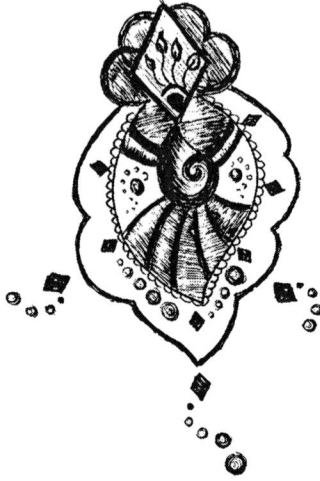

The Blue Door

"He that has eyes to see and ears to hear may convince himself that no mortal can keep a secret. If his lips are silent, he chatters with his fingertips; betrayal oozes out of him at every pore."

—Sigmund Freud
(*Analysis of a Case of Hysteria*)

Jennifer was the first to head for the lobby. She had thought about stopping off at Adriana's room but then decided against it, not knowing if she were still asleep or not. She had been thinking about those wonderful hammocks in the lobby. Jennifer wondered why she had never seen anyone sitting on them. This would be her chance to relax on one while waiting for the others.

The door of the elevator opened. Jennifer hesitated for a moment, not recognizing the surroundings in front of her. Was she on the wrong floor? Was this the same lobby they had walked through the night before? Stepping out slowly from the elevator, she started looking around. Yes, it was the same lobby, but so much more magnificent and breath-taking with the sunlight playing on the walls. It looked like a mini-paradise filled with beautiful flowers and plants as far as the eye could see. Exotic birds perched on treetops whistling magical tunes almost in unison with one another.

The air was so fragrant and sweet, bringing all the whispers of the flowers to the senses. The sound of the waterfall soothed the soul, calmed the mind and relaxed the body as it gracefully poured into the small pond below. The water was like a 'touchless' massage as she passed in front of it.

Jennifer looked around for the hammocks. They were neatly tucked away amongst the vegetation. Just as she was ready to hop on one, she saw Magic almost gliding towards her. She knelt on the floor, calling the stunning creature to her. Magic stopped a few feet away from Jennifer and just stared at her. She felt paralyzed by the cat's gaze.

"Good morning Jennifer, did you sleep well?"

Jennifer looked around to see who was talking to her, but then she had not really heard a voice. It was more like vibrations had passed through her mind, but nevertheless she looked behind her to double check that no one was there.

"Jennifer, don't be afraid. I'm the one talking to you. Magic. Look at me please. You don't have to talk out loud, just think about what you'd like to say and I'll understand."

"You talk, Magic?!" She thought.

"Yes Jennifer, among some other things that you'll soon experience for yourself," Magic replied, *"Go ahead and lie down on the hammock. I'm going to take you on a little trip."*

Magic walked towards the hammock and waited for Jennifer to get over her initial shock.

"Lie down, close your eyes and think back to the time you went to visit Austria with your parents."

Jennifer did just that. She sunk into the hammock, letting her mind venture to that time so many years ago. She closed her eyes and took in a deep breath, thinking about her trip.

Jennifer felt as if she were moving, floating in a way. She felt a bit uneasy and out of control as the hammock swung back and forth, so she decided to open her eyes. She suddenly noticed that she was no longer in the lobby of The Karma Hotel. She was standing outside of the same hotel she and her parents had stayed at all those years before. She looked around for Magic, needing a familiar face to regain her composure, to make her feel safe. Jennifer was not scared—on the contrary, she was overtaken by exhilaration and anticipation. Just then, she felt Magic weaving in and out between her feet.

"Magic, there you are!" She said, feeling relieved, "Thank God I found you. Where are we?"

"Oh Jennifer, you know exactly where we are. The question is what would you like to do now?"

"Well, the last time I was here, I asked my parents if I could go visit my old house. You see I was convinced I lived here before."

"Yes, I know. I'm aware of that. So let's take a little walk." The cat turned gracefully and started walking up the street as Jennifer followed.

No one really noticed them appear out of the blue, nor were Jennifer and Magic too concerned with her obviously different attire from the rest of the people in Salzburg. She deducted that it could not have been the same year she left the Hotel, judging from the way the people were dressed. Had they traveled back in time?

They walked along the cobbled road, as if they had walked that same route a thousand times before. It felt so familiar. They must have been in a very affluent area; the houses were magnificent and regal looking. Jennifer stopped in front of one of the mansions. She kept blinking as if she had something in her eyes.

"Are you all right Jennifer?" Magic whispered, "What's the matter?"

"Nothing Magic, I just keep getting these flashbacks, these images of a woman from a different era, all dressed up and fancy looking. I don't know if it's me. I can't see her face. But I feel connected to her, in a very strange way," She answered.

"Good, then the process is working. Continue."

"This is the house, Magic. I don't know how we ended up here, or how you knew, but I'm sure this is where I used to live." Jennifer spoke with such certainty.

"That's wonderful, Jennifer. Now I want you to walk up to the porch, touch the front door, and marvel at the images that will come your way."

"Images?" She questioned …

"I'll wait for you here. Go my curious one; you've waited too long for this."

Jennifer could not contain her excitement anymore. She ran up to the front of the house and reached for the entrance. She pressed her palms firmly against the beautifully decorated wooden door. Suddenly, some recognizable but mostly unfamiliar scenes and pictures were attacking her mind. She saw herself playing hopscotch with Sally—the little girl who lived next door—her mother giving her a bath, her first day at school, and climbing trees with her cousins. Those familiar visions soon faded, being replaced by the woman she had seen earlier in her mind, such a beautiful woman who was obviously an upper-class member of society, reeking of flair and elegance. Yet the woman looked so sad and lonely.

Jennifer started feeling the stranger's pain, her despair. Her whole body began to ache. She felt nauseous and dizzy. She tried to disconnect herself from this woman, from the images, but could not. Jennifer and the woman became one and the same. Even though the two women were from different times and dimensions, she felt as if she had become her, and the miserable woman had become Jennifer.

Every atom and cell of her body felt occupied. Suddenly she pulled back from the door and let out an ear-piercing scream. She fell to the floor, crying and shaking from the experience.

"Jennifer, relax my darling! Sit back and take a deep breath. I promise nothing will happen to you. You are completely safe. Please close your eyes."

Her eyes were closed already, and she was too afraid to open them, too afraid to witness anymore awful images. She felt Magic close to her and heard the bells chiming around his neck. She felt him jump onto her chest. She started stroking him, but she still kept her eyes closed.

"Tell me what happened Jennifer—what did you see?" Magic asked.

"Oh Magic, it was awful!" Jennifer opened her eyes immediately, realizing she had returned to the hotel. It was as if the flowers were aware of her terrible ordeal and had released the most heavenly scent into the air to calm and welcome her back to the present.

"What was awful, Jenny? Talk to me."

"This poor woman, she was so depressed and sad. I could sense an ache so deep within her. It was as if her soul were crying out to me, crying tears of blood and despair."

She wiped her own tears away with her shirtsleeve as she went on:

"Then, just as I was about to pull away, I saw her hanging herself. She stood up on a chair, and then she just stepped off. It happened in that same house, Magic. I'm sure it did! Who is she, Magic? Why did I feel almost possessed by her? Why couldn't I disconnect from the images earlier?"

Jennifer looked so distressed and confused as she tried to make some sense of what had just happened.

"Calm down my sweet one. You did beautifully. Let me try to explain what happened. We traveled back to a very significant time in one of your lives. You see, sometimes people experience a smooth ride when being taken to certain places and time periods.

"It may take only a few seconds to make a connection to the images presented to them. Meanwhile, others need to be more patient and accepting of the often difficult and disturbing scenes that find them."

Magic continued:

"Your journey of spiritual exploration might be more complicated and sensitive than we both thought. But that's why you are here, Jennifer. You will always be guided and supported during each move you make to get a step closer to finding the answers to your unresolved questions."

"So you don't know who she was? Jennifer asked.

Of course Magic knew, dear reader. Everyone at The Karma Hotel was aware of all the particulars regarding each guest, especially Rhea. She envisaged their lives, past and present as if she were watching a documentary. Each story would tell itself, dance in her mind until she was completely aware of their predicament.

"Let the story tell itself, Jennifer. There is a wealth of details, different angles that you'll soon discover. I would dilute the experience for you if I were to simply state the answer to your question. It is your task to discover the truth. No one should interfere with that process, not even I."

"I understand Magic, thank you. It just seemed so real—such a part of me!"

"It was very real my dear, as real as a cat having a conversation with you, as I am right now."

This cat even had a sense of humor?! Jennifer laughed. A feeling of calmness swept over her. Her anxiety was slowly abandoning her soul.

"You must hurry now; the others are waiting for you through the blue door."

Magic turned to face one of the massive doors on the far left side of the Lobby.

"Remember to keep this our little secret. Good luck with the rest of your adventure."

"Thank you Magic, I'll see you later."

Jennifer turned around and walked towards the blue door. It was not completely closed, so she pushed it open and saw the others all sitting in a circle on the floor, with Rhea in the middle. Had they walked by her in the lobby? Had they noticed her?

Just then, as if he had read her mind, Alexander said, "Hey Jenny, we saw you on that hammock. Was it comfy?"

"Yeah it was, very comfy and scary at the same time."

Jennifer looked at Rhea for any signs that might show she was aware of her voyage with Magic. Rhea acknowledged her question with a wink.

"You looked so relaxed, we didn't want to bother you," said Adriana

"Welcome Jennifer," said Rhea, "Please join us. We haven't begun yet—I was just asking our friends how they enjoyed their first night with us. But now that you're here, we may begin."

Rhea continued: "Adam has prepared a scrumptious brunch for us, so let's help ourselves to the wonderful medley of cuisine prepared especially for you."

"Excellent, I'm starving!" said Daniel.

Everyone made their way to the buffet table placed at the far corner. This room was even more beautiful than the one they had met in last night. It was so exclusively decorated, with many different colors and patterns employed throughout the room, mostly geometric shapes and designs. Huge cushions were thrown in five different clusters throughout. After walking around and chatting to each other for awhile, they each grabbed a plate and started to fill it with all the delicious dishes prepared for them. Alexander and Jennifer sat together, while Rhea, Daniel and Adriana went to another set of cushions nearby.

How were these foods prepared? What kinds of spices were used? Each morsel, each bite tasted different, an infinite reservoir of sensations. The food danced with their taste buds, tempted them to have more. Daniel had always been a fussy eater, but there was nothing on the table he chose not to try and enjoy. Alexander filled his plate up three times before he decided he was on the verge of explosion if he had another bite. Jennifer and Adriana asked Rhea if they could talk to Adam about getting the recipes of these beautifully prepared dishes.

"You think Adam might reveal his secrets to us, Rhea?" Adriana asked teasingly.

"You can try to ask, but I'm sure he'll refuse to disclose the methods of his inventions," replied Rhea, "Even if he does tell you, believe me, certain secret ingredients will be left out. Even I don't know what they are!"

Rhea took in another mouth full of the heavenly chocolate mousse.

"I believe it! I feel drunk after this meal," Alexander said, "Not even drunk, kind of elevated. Is that normal?"

Just then Adam walked into the room. They all stood up to greet him.

"Yes, it is normal Alexander," Adam quickly responded, "I've put together these dishes to bring about the exact feeling you just described, 'elevated'."

"Then you have succeeded, Adam. I can't get enough!" said Jennifer.

"And no, you may not have the recipes!" said Adam humorously, knowing that most of their guests asked for instructions on how to prepare the food.

"Now, be nice Adam," said Rhea, "Maybe we can give them an idea of how to replicate some of these delectable dishes."

"Well, alright. Just before their departure, after they've tried all the meals, I'll disclose one recipe to you each. Maybe!"

The guests all looked pleased at the thought of being let into Adam's magical world, to be allowed one step closer to understanding the multitude of variables that must have been used in his creations.

"I'd like you all to take a walk around the grounds for about an hour," said Rhea, "You may go together or alone; it's up to you. But please meet me again in the lobby for the next stage of your journey."

Each of the guests agreed, thanked Adam for the meal once again and headed out of the hotel. They decided to wander around separately. There was so much to see and enjoy. Each person proceeded in a different direction. Adriana especially needed this time alone. She missed Stephen immeasurably. This must have been the first time she had not spoken to him for so long.

They did not see each other often, but they talked three or four times a day. He would send her romantic cards and letters filled with words of love and longing. He had such a wonderful way with words; they seemed to love him and to gather around his thoughts, waiting to be chosen. Each letter, each expression made her fall deeper in love with him.

Stephen's words pierced deeply into Adriana's heart, begging to live there forever. They left her breathless, unable to focus or think about anyone else but him. Adriana needed him in her life, to love and worship, as desperately as she needed to breathe. Was he too good to be true? Had she created this imaginary lover in her mind? Could he turn out to be like every other worthless man to whom she had given her heart?

There was so much mystery and so many unanswered questions shrouding their relationship. Although certain of his feelings for her, that he did indeed love her, she still wasn't sure how deep those feelings ran. And if he did love her as intensely as he claimed to love her so often when they were together, then she wondered again about why Stephen was not hers to have entirely to herself.

Adriana could see Magic walking towards her at a distance. She dismissed her negative thoughts as she watched the white puffball glide charmingly towards her. She knelt down to pet Magic, and he immediately jumped onto her lap. The cat purred loudly as Adriana pet him.

"You miss him Adriana, don't you? Magic whispered.

Shocked by what she had heard, Adriana jumped to standing position.

"Who's that? Who said that?" She said as she looked all around her.

"I did." Thought Magic, *"I know how much Stephen means to you, Adriana."*

"Oh my God, you can't talk. You're a cat!" She said.

"I can, believe in me, and please make a wish. Think carefully about what you would like to wish for."

"This is amazing, Magic! You know I always thought my cat used to understand me? I would talk to her for hours, but she never replied," Adriana reflected.

"Maybe you weren't listening carefully enough."

"Yes, maybe you're right. So I can make any wish and you'll make it come true?"

"That's right. Take your time. Whisper the words in your mind and close your eyes while repeating your wish."

She did just that, closed her eyes tightly and repeated these words: "I wish to be where Stephen is right now, to see him with his wife, at home. To get a glimpse of what his other life is like."

"Open your eyes, Adriana," Magic communicated to her, silently.

She opened her eyes and suddenly there was Stephen sitting on the couch, watching TV. Was this his house, his living room?

"Yes it is. Now remember, he can't see or hear us. You're here only to observe," he said, answering her questions.

Adriana watched Stephen so intently. God, how she wanted to reach out and hold him in her arms. He looked so sad, so lonely, not at all like the person she knew. Where was his lively spirit, his infectious smile? Just then, a woman walked into the room. That must be his wife, she thought.

"Yes it is his wife. Is she how you imagined her to be?"

"Not at all Magic. She's so much more beautiful. He never really talks about her, but somehow I thought she would be very simple, maybe even unattractive."

But she was not. Indeed, Stephen's wife was a striking woman. She walked into the room and sat next to Stephen.

"Hey, how are you?" his wife asked.

"Good, and you?" he returned the question.

"Not bad."

"That's good to hear."

"Is it?" his wife enquired.

"Yes, why wouldn't it be?"

"Do you really care about how I am?"

"Ok, where is this discussion going?" asked Stephen, "Do you have something you'd like to talk about?"

Stephen looked obviously irritated and seemed so indifferent and detached that Adriana found it difficult to accept that this was the same passionate, tender, lively man she was in love with. She started wondering how Stephen and his wife ever got together. Were they always this cold with one another, or had they become this way due to the demands of life and marriage?

What is it about this age-old institution that imprisons lovers? Does the formula of passion and intimacy somehow get altered once two people have signed on the dotted line? Should we accept Shakespeare's opinion that passionate love has to be unrequited or unconsummated or it would spin down to family tragedy and suicide, to the deaths of the lovers? I don't think so, dear wonderer. Keep looking for your own other half, for the one to compliment who you are with their very being; perhaps Shakespeare was merely not so lucky in love.

Adriana returned her attention to the couple.

"No where—the conversation is going no where," replied his wife, taking a deep sigh. "It's just that I'm sick of seeing you sitting on that couch."

"You didn't seem to mind too much last night when you walked in at four in the morning," Stephen snapped back angrily.

"Do you want to go out for dinner?" his wife asked, completely ignoring his comment.

"No, not really. I have some work I need to finish."

Adriana thought how different they were from one another. Of course she hadn't observed them long enough to comment on their compatibility, but there was no doubt regarding this couple's unhappiness.

"Magic, he looks so miserable," Adriana remarked, "It kills me to see him like this."

"I know it does, but you spent so many sleepless nights wondering about his relationship with his wife. It was about time you saw for yourself, to ease your soul a little," Magic replied.

"So why does he stay with her?" Questioned Adriana, "I mean, this is such a miserable existence!"

Somehow she felt even more bewildered after seeing Stephen at home with his wife. At least previously she could convince herself that he had a somewhat loving relationship with his wife, and that was one of the major reasons he would not leave her.

Stephen got up from the couch and walked into the other room. Magic and Adriana followed quietly, invisibly. This must have been his study. He walked over to his desk, opened the drawer and took out a picture from in between one of his books. It was a picture of Adriana. He kissed it, inhaled her imaginary scent from the photo and placed it against his chest. What he uttered next cut through her soul like a blunt knife.

"Some people live their entire lives without falling in love. I have lived my life and I fell in love. God I'm ready to leave now ..."

"Magic, enough! I can't bear to see him hurting like this anymore," Adriana said, now almost in tears.

"I know it's difficult Adriana, but you needed to see that he is deeply in love with you. You must never question his love or intentions towards you

again. Now close your eyes. It's time for us to go back. The remaining pieces of the puzzle will be brought to you soon."

"I hope so, Magic," She replied, "This confusion about the reason Fate has tempted me with the man of my dreams, yet she won't surrender him to me completely, is killing me."

Adriana closed her eyes and let out a deep sigh. She hoped Magic had not seen the tears rolling down her cheeks as she thought about the words Stephen had whispered, but at the same time, she felt comforted by the fact that Stephen truly loved her and longed for her with an intensity to equal her love for him.

"Hey Adriana, wake up. It's time to go back inside," Alexander said while patting her on the shoulder to wake her up.

"I'm sorry; I didn't realize I had fallen asleep. How long have I been here?" She asked.

"Not long, perhaps only for a few minutes," replied Alexander, "Rhea called out for us earlier. Apparently they're ready to begin."

Alexander helped Adriana to her feet. She took a few seconds to regain consciousness and to collect her thoughts. She knew she had seen Stephen; it surely could not have been just a dream, could it? Alexander and Adriana walked towards the hotel, meeting the others at the entrance.

"I think Rhea said to wait for her here," said Jennifer.

Right on cue, Rhea appeared in the lobby, signaling her guests to join her near the glass door.

The Glass Door

"I hope you enjoyed your stroll through the grounds; it's beautiful this time of the year, don't you think?" Rhea asked, smiling generously at her guests.

"Follow me towards the glass door please," She continued, "It's time to begin. Now the reason this door is made of glass is because of the character of the material used. Glass is transparent yet it acts as a sort of boundary.

"One can see through it but may remain within the safe confines of the other side, separated from what is being observed. This is where your journey will begin. You will glimpse 'the other side,' gain some insight, and more knowledge regarding some of the questions you have concerning the issues you're experiencing in this life," She explained.

The guests all listened carefully and were excited about the prospects of this next stage. Rhea led them through the door. They walked behind her; uncertain about what they would find in the room or on the 'other side'—neither destination seeming more important than the other.

The room was decorated in light pastel colors ranging from soft pinks to subtle yellows, to baby blues. Jennifer thought about how much the room resembled a child's nursery. Maybe that of twins, a boy and a girl, since a range of both blue and pink was incorporated. How appropriate that she would draw upon this analogy because this next part of their journey was about going back to beginnings, perhaps even regressing back to infancy to gain a deeper understanding of themselves. Possibly, they would go even further than infancy, into a previous life.

There were four main areas within this room, each closed off by a separate door. In the middle of the area, surrounded by the four doors, was a round table with six chairs that were carefully arranged with equal distance between each of their places. This room was smaller, less formal and obtrusive compared to the huge dining room they had sat in the previous evening.

"Please take a seat," Rhea said.

They did as she instructed, with Rhea still standing, leaving two chairs empty.

"Each chair is a different color, as I'm sure you've noticed by now. This is the way we decide which room you'll enter for your first private consultation, since the rooms are colored in the exact shade of the chairs you occupy."

Upon hearing Rhea's words, each one of the guests turned around to see the color of chair they had chosen. Adriana was sitting on a baby pink shade, and Alexander on the apple green shade; Jennifer had chosen the pale yellow seat, and Daniel the light purple chair.

Are you thinking the same thing I'm thinking, fellow voyagers? Had they unconsciously or consciously chosen the same color seat as their rooms? Let me save you the burden of turning back my pages to answer this question. Yes, they had, however none of them would think about this until they got back to their rooms that night.

"All colors possess a unique energy," accentuated Rhea, "We are highly drawn to and influenced by this force. Instead of assigning rooms at this stage, we prefer you to choose the energy that attracts you the most. You have done so by selecting the chairs around this table."

Rhea examined the expression on their faces. She was used to the silence surrounding her visitors at this point. She knew they were listening, eager to learn more, rather than filling up the atmosphere with chatty nonsense.

Just then, Chance walked into the room carrying a beautiful, yet ancient looking bag. It looked like a second grader had made it for a class project, as if patches of different materials had been randomly glued together to form the mysterious vessel. Curiously, it looked quite durable judging from the number of contents trying to break through—unsuccessfully. Chance kept switching it from one hand to another, presumably to give each arm a break from the labor of toting the bag.

"Hi everyone, I'm sorry if I'm late. This bag has a mind of its own. It refused to cooperate with me and kept hiding all the little bits and pieces I needed to bring today," Chance highlighted, totally oblivious to the reactions of her clients.

"Everyone's a little wacko around here, don't you think?" Daniel whispered to Alexander.

"No, not 'wacko' Daniel. Let's use another word. How about special, enchanted or 'amagtic'!!" Alexander suggested.

"'Amagtic'? What does that mean?"

"I just made it up. It's a combination of amazing, magical and fantastic—amagtic!"

"Ok Alexander, whatever! I think you've been here too long already!"

Alexander looked out towards the window and saw Magic sprawled out on the grass, soaking in the rays. Magic turned his head and held Alexander's stare.

"I love that word, Alexander. Well done. I'll surely add it to my vocabulary," Magic whispered.

Alexander turned to Daniel, who was talking to Jennifer as Adriana was talking to Chance and Rhea. So where was that voice coming from? Alexander suddenly panicked and thought Daniel was probably right! He was losing it! Now he was hearing voices?

"No Alexander, never give into skepticism. You have never done so throughout your life, so why begin now, when at the most enchanting place in our galaxy? Magic whispered.

"Who is that? Who's talking to me?' Alexander whispered back in his thoughts.

"Look down towards the floor. It's me, Magic."

Sure enough, Alexander looked down and saw Magic, weaving in and out between his legs.

"Hi Magic, how are you?"

"I'm fine, Alexander. You don't seem shocked about a cat talking to you."

"No, I'm not shocked at all. I knew you were special from the first time I saw you."

Alexander simply dismissed this unusual encounter as another miraculous trait of The Karma Hotel.

"I've always had an extraordinary bond with cats. I never spoke to one, but they seem to understand me," emphasized Alexander.

"Maybe you were one of us in a past life!"

"Maybe, but somehow I don't think it's that. It must be something deeper, more complex."

"You're right, it is Alexander. Now what I'd like you to do is think back to a difficult time in your life, a situation that was somehow left unresolved. I think I know what it is, but I need you to affirm it before taking you there."

Alexander paused for a moment to think about the most significant event he'd like to return to.

"Alright, I'd like to go back to when I was 20, to have a chance to talk to my best friend who committed suicide that year."

"I thought as much. Close your eyes please, let's go and see Damon."

Damon, how close Alexander had been to him. He thought about all the great times they had with one another. All those nights they spent sitting with friends, drinking coffee, listening to music and talking about how they could make the world a better place. Damon was always the negative introvert. Alexander, on the opposite end of the spectrum, was the positive extrovert.

However, somehow their differences brought them closer together, creating a richer friendship.

Nevertheless, Damon and Alexander were not necessarily influenced by one another in terms of greatly changing their perceptions about the world—but they did learn a great deal from each other. Damon tried endlessly to warn Alexander about people taking advantage of his generous nature. He would tell him to wake up to the dark side of the world and stop being so selfless. In return, Alexander tried to show Damon the beautiful side of life, struggling to exemplify the world through a more positive image.

Alexander knew Damon had issues with himself, his past and family members. He tried relentlessly to help him overcome those obstacles that were polluting his chances for happiness in the present. He begged him to seek professional help. Damon promised he would, just as soon as he had some time. Unfortunately, that time never came. Damon committed suicide by drowning himself in the bath the night before his 21st birthday. No pills, no drugs, no overdose, no slit wrists, no ropes—just an innocent looking bathing appliance turned into his death chamber.

Alexander had been the one to find him the next day. He had gone over to Damon's apartment to invite him out for breakfast. The image of his best friend lying dead and bloated in the bath would haunt him forever. Even now as he thought about that devastating morning, he was once again struck by the overwhelming sense of loss and sadness he had felt. He had so many questions to ask, mainly about why Damon had chosen to end his life rather than battle through this war we are all a part of.

"That's exactly why I've brought you here. To ask him this question that's been troubling you," said Magic.

"I tried so hard to help him try to deal with all the problems he had."

"I know you did, Alexander. But sometimes we all need to let others fight their own battles, no matter how close they are to us. Or else we end up spreading ourselves thin and only living a fraction of a life rather than a whole one.

"Happiness can't come from an outside source. It must be found within the individual. This way, we are not dependant on a situation or a person to feel happy; happiness will always exist.'

"Hey Alex, what's up?" Alexander opened his eyes, recognized what used to be his friend's apartment, looked around and found Damon sitting on the couch.

Only Damon and his mom ever called him Alex.

"Hey Damon, how have you been?" Alexander couldn't believe how real this situation seemed. As if time had stopped, the place was unchanged and two friends were meeting as they had always met. Maybe it was real.

"Not too bad, buddy. You know, still struggling."

"Magic, does he know he's dead?"

"Yes, and he knows you are alive. He wanted this meeting as much as you did. Be as frank and open as you like with him. What's wrong with you? Have you forgotten how close you two were?"

Alexander shifted his attention back to his friend.

"Struggling with what Damon?" asked Alexander.

"Well, you know those guys up there don't really approve of suicide."

"Which guys?"

"You know, the welcoming committee!" Damon accentuated in his usual sarcastic tone, "When you die Alex, it's not like you float on clouds, angels feeding you grapes while you hear harps being played in the background! At least that wasn't my experience. Knowing you, that's probably what your welcoming committee will be like!"

"So tell me more. This is fascinating. What's the struggle about? Do you have to face some kind of punishment?"

"No, not really. There's no such thing as punishment up there. It's more about learning lessons. They're upset with me because I took the easy way out, before conquering my demons. So I have to spend a lot of time thinking about my Earthly actions and what I could have done differently."

"Could I have helped more Damon? Could I have been a better friend? Why didn't you tell me the extent of your despair? For God's sake, Damon, why didn't you let me save you?"

"Alex, you were more than a brother to me; there's nothing you could have done. I didn't want to live anymore; it's as simple as that. I never shared your love for life, no matter how hard I tried. My demons just kept catching up to me. But I wish I had been a better friend to you. I'm sorry if I constantly acted like a wet blanket on your soul. Please forgive me."

"You don't need to apologize, buddy. I knew what you were going through at least to some extent. You'll make it up to me when we both come back as dogs in our next life!"

"Well, I'm going to be one nasty dog! Apparently I'll have to come back later in another life to deal with all these unresolved issues. You might have to wait a few lives before I make it up to you."

"I'll be looking forward to that day. After all, what are friends for?"

"I'll find you Alex, I promise, and maybe then I can give back a little of what you gave me for so many years."

Damon walked towards Alexander, putting his arm around his best friend.

"Thank you, Damon. I'm so happy we had this chance to talk."

"The name's not Damon; it's Daniel!! How many times do I have to tell you?"

When Alexander opened his eyes again, he found himself sitting at the round table in the pastel room with the others. He was no longer embracing his old friend; instead he was transported back to reality by a dose of Daniel's agitation.

"Sorry Daniel. What did you say?" Alexander asked.

"You keep calling me Damon, and my name's Daniel, remember?" Daniel explained, very irritably.

Alexander looked around once again, trying to make sense of what had just happened. He saw Magic strolling towards the door leading into the garden. Before he had a chance to figure out what had just occurred, if anything at all, Rhea started addressing the group again.

"Good afternoon Chance. You look ravishing today, as always. I'll have a talk with your bag as soon as we finish here. I know what it might need," Rhea said.

"Thank you, Rhea. You might be more successful than I in trying to get through to it! So, what have I missed?" asked Chance.

"Well, now that we're all here,' Rhea said winking at Alexander, "let me remind you of what I was saying. Chance, I was just telling our friends about colors and their powers. They've chosen their seats according to the color they felt most drawn to, so I think we can begin."

The wink from Rhea was exactly what Alexander needed at that moment to dispel his doubts about seeing Damon. His return to the Hotel had been so swift, leaving him no time to distinguish between the two dimensions.

"Wonderful, I'm ready when you are," Chance replied.

"So, Chance is the resident psychic right?" asked Adriana.

"That's right Adriana, to say the least. However, she is capable of so much more. Chance possesses skills and talents that have never been labeled before and are unique to her and The Karma Hotel," said Rhea.

"Yes, a psychic," Chance agreed, "but I'm also known as a medium, spiritual communicator, clairvoyant and karmic astrologer. The way I work, my preference, is to let these talents find me as we progress in our session. I don't like to talk about what they are, or make any promises regarding the findings or outcome. The powers above us will determine how much they want me to know, and more importantly, how much I should reveal to you. Each reading is distinctive, as is the person being read for," Chance said.

"Wow, ok, sounds great," Adriana said.

"You will each meet Chance in your designated rooms, separately. The duration of the session may differ, ranging anywhere from half an hour to an hour, depending on the issues that might surface. You are welcome to stay here together while waiting your turn. However, when the reading is complete, you are advised to go back up to your room to write about the findings as the second entry in your journal, while the experience is still unmarked in your thoughts."

Getting up from her seat to prepare the first room where Chance and Alexander would begin their session, Rhea wrapped up by asking the eager guests if they had any questions. She could feel their restless energy mounting up. It's only natural; they had waited so many years to have their perplexing dilemmas clarified.

⁛⁛⁛⁛

Chance

"*With memory set smarting like a reopened wound, a man's past is not simply a dead history, an outworn preparation of the present: it is not a repented error shaken loose from the life: it is a still quivering part of himself, bringing shudders and bitter flavors and the tingling of a merited shame.*"

—George Elliot (*Middlemarch*)

In order to prepare adequately for her session, Chance always engaged in a set of rituals before beginning a reading. She proceeded to the first room while Rhea finished explaining the logistics of this next stage. She placed her bag on the round table, dimmed the lights and arranged her chair so she would be directly facing the other person. She took out her Tarot cards, her multi-colored candles and an ancient looking piece of paper that looked like it had survived many adventures and voyages.

Chance set her cards aside and began reading from the paper. The title clearly stated the intent of the words to follow: *A magic spell to rebalance the body, mind and spirit.* She reached into her bag and pulled out a long white feather, got up from her seat, moved towards the clear part of the room and began walking in a clockwise direction. After making a complete circle, she then stopped and placed her feather on the floor beneath her.

Chance moved towards the table, reached into her bag and carefully took out a beautiful long stemmed rose. Again, she walked towards the spot where she had placed her feather on the floor and sat down, placing the rose next to it. She reached into her pocket, taking out an exquisitely intricate lace handkerchief. She proceeded to pick up the feather and the rose, wrapped the handkerchief around the two items, and placed the neat sachet back on the floor.

Chance then closed her eyes and took three deep breaths. She cleared all her thoughts of pedantic issues and concentrated on grounding herself to the exact spot that she had chosen. She thought about the air that flowed into her lungs, the same air common to all living beings. She reflected on love, life and the power of the spirit world. As she exhaled the last deep breath, she looked up at the ceiling and said:

"With the help of this feather, assist me in flying to you. Help me gain more insight into the tribulations that continue to disturb our friends. With the help of this rose, let their problems dissolve, blossoming into solutions, beckoning a season of change, a season of renewal and of bright beginnings. Without you I am both deaf and blind. Show me the way; whisper to me your wise and worthy prophecies."

As always, after this ritual, tears started flowing down her face. She felt so honored to be blessed by such a gift, so special that the powers above used her as a means to transmit their messages to those too preoccupied to listen. If only the souls on Earth were more in tune with their spiritual guides. If only they would pay attention and trust the voices from within.

Dear reader, perhaps it is important we think about at what point we learn to ignore the astute advice of our spirit guides? Why is it that we would rather follow the recommendations of a stranger than rely on our own intuition? Find refuge and all the answers within the heart of your heart next time you're in need of guidance, my dear companion. Only you and your twin soul hold the manual to your happiness.

ഔരുഔരുഔരുഔരു

Alexander

Alexander made his way towards the room. He could see Chance sitting on the floor. He hesitated to enter the room because she looked so occupied and distant. Just as he was about to turn around, Chance turned her attention to Alexander, as if she had read his mind. Immediately she noticed his clear blue eyes, the kind of eyes that penetrate your soul and observe things that go totally unnoticed by other people.

"Come in Alexander. I'm ready to begin," she said, unable to pull away from the gravitation of his stare.

"Thank you. I'm sorry if I interrupted your thoughts," He said, while pulling out the chair opposite hers.

"There are no interruptions at all, only new situations," She replied, "Please take a seat. Now I want you to take three deep breathes and ground yourself as much as you can. Imagine you are a tree needing to plant your roots into the ground. Concentrate and think about this exercise, make it happen in your mind."

This was the same activity with which all of her clients began. This was her opportunity to get a feel for their energy, their anxiety and any other vibes that might be evident.

Alexander did feel grounded and relaxed, as Chance had promised. He was thoroughly engaged in the process.

"Good, we may begin now. I want you to listen carefully, but stop me to ask questions whenever you need. Since this is a past life examination, we'll start by looking at your present existence in the hope that the details of one or other past lives will slowly start to be revealed."

The candle in the middle of the table flickered in agreement.

"I don't believe in talking too much about the future, given that it will not help us here today. Not yet anyway," She said and Alexander nodded.

"These are magical cards Alexander," Chance almost whispered these words as if hiding a secret from the walls, "Love and respect them as I do. Shuffle them slowly in any direction you wish, keeping in mind any concerns you may have. Then place them on the table, spread them out and choose twelve cards from the pile."

Chance asked her clients to choose the cards, but she knew it was the cards that chose the person being read for. The cards were as eager to be revealed as the client was to have a reading. But she kept that to herself. To divulge that little piece of information would be the same as a magician revealing the secrets behind his tricks, the magic would dissipate and all that would remain would be a parlor trick.

Alexander picked out twelve cards and placed them upright on the table. The beautiful pictures told a story only Chance was able to hear. She watched Alexander as he tried to make sense of the images on the table. She felt he had some psychic abilities but had never worked on developing them further.

"Alexander, you're truly a unique soul, an older soul if I may add. There are different levels of souls you see, and I get the feeling you've been among us for a very long time." She studied each card before speaking.

"You are such a generous person, so giving and kind, and you have always been there for loved ones, from a very young age, always putting yourself second to their needs. You're also wonderful at your job, involving some kind of charity or social work.

"Yes, that's right. You chose an occupation in which you can continue to help people less fortunate than yourself. You're sense of achievement and happiness comes from improving the lives of other people. Is this making sense to you?" She looked up at him only long enough to ask the question.

Yes, it makes perfect sense," he said, thinking no other psychic had ever began a reading so accurately.

"The people you work with love you whole-heartedly. You have saved the lives of many people, given them hope for tomorrow, restoring their faith in life, love and humanity." She paused for a moment allowing Alexander to think back to Wanda.

Wanda was one of the people Alexander had touched with his rare gift. It was because of his attention and unconditional love that she felt the desire to live after years of just existing.

"Yes, just like what you did for Wanda."

Alexander looked up in amazement as Chance said those words.

"You touched her life in a very special way. You know that she's playing the piano again and has just released her debut CD?" She asked.

"Of course you know, because it was dedicated to you, wasn't it?" Alexander nodded with a heartfelt smile.

Wanda had sent him a copy of her CD as soon as it was completed.

"But there's something else here, almost like a gray cloud that weaves in and out of your life periodically. I use the term gray cloud as a metaphor to describe these intense periods of depression or anxiety that attack you with no warning at all."

Chance looked away from Alexander and the cards, seeming suddenly confused. Her eyes darted from left to right, as if reading imaginary words or looking at images floating around the room. Alexander watched as she shifted her attention back to the cards.

"No, I wouldn't call it depression. It's more a deep sorrow or guilt that attacks you, shuts you down. Is this making any sense?" She asked, looking straight through his eyes and into his soul.

"Now it is," replied Alexander, "I didn't want to interrupt you when you said 'periods of depression.' My condition is much more complex than that, more like the way you described it right now, as sorrow and guilt, and there is even an element of fear of some sort," Alexander said.

"I understand. I also see how much you've suffered as a result of these periods of emotional siege. This is why we've brought you here Alexander, isn't it?" Chance asked.

"Yes, it is. I need to know why this unexplainable force, that leaves me incapacitated, attacks me so often."

"Well, I have some idea about what might be going on, but in order to get a more accurate reading, let's ask the cards through a specific layout made for uncovering past lives."

"All right, sounds good to me. How many cards shall I choose?"

"21," Chance answered, including at the end, and never forgetting, "please."

Chance closed her eyes and pleaded with her guides to shed some more light on what was troubling Alexander. Being a more advanced soul meant that he had gone through many lives and incarnations; however, she was only interested in the time and existence that a lesson was not completely learned. She was only interested in the same life that was distracting his present time on earth. She asked Alexander to layout the cards he'd chosen in the shape of a tree. Each card, each part of that tree told a piece of the story.

"Now Alexander, I can only help open the door to a troubled past. The information we uncover can be used to trigger your imbedded memory of that life. Then Latifah and Dameer, through their own specific methods, will help you unravel the story further. Is that clear?"

"Yes, I understand."

"I also want you to concentrate on the details I'll be exposing. Try and imagine yourself as the main character of that narrative, however bizarre and nonsensical it may seem. Think back to any dreams or flashbacks you may have had anytime in your life related to our reading." Once again, Chance directed her attention to the cards.

"We're being taken back in time. I'm not sure exactly to when, maybe around the late 1600s. We're in Europe, in England to be more precise. I sense poverty and hunger on your part. Oh, that's interesting. You're a woman in this life."

Chance diverted her gaze to the second card.

"A very strong and determined woman if I may add. Somehow, you're different than the other ladies of that time. You're unmarried and live alone, but you have a very caring and positive energy surrounding you.

"You're not at all bitter about being underprivileged. Have I hit any trigger buttons yet? Can you relate to anything I've said so far?" She looked up at Alexander, waiting for an acknowledgment.

"No Chance, not yet."

"That's ok. Let's continue. The scent of herbs and spices flow liberally around your home. I see hundreds of bottles placed around on tables and shelves, each labeled in white. I get the feeling you must have been some kind of chef, a professional one judging from the ingredients and the appliances throughout the house."

Chance's eyes kept shifting from side to side as she spoke. Suddenly, she looked up from the cards, stared out into space and began speaking to what Alex thought was herself, but actually she was talking to her guides.

"I know, I know. Something doesn't fit. The picture is just too somber and distinctive to be referred to in that sense. There's something more going on than just cooking here. Talk to me please. What is it?" She shot her attention back to Alex, instructing him to pick out two more cards from the deck.

"I knew it. Now it makes more sense. Why couldn't you have come to us earlier?" Chance addressed the two cards as casually as if talking to long lost friends."

'The Magician' and the 'The High Priestess' had made their entrance, bringing with them missing pieces of the puzzle.

"Alexander, you were no average cook my dear. I get the feeling you were some kind of healer, a druggist perhaps, however rare that it was for women to be in those days. Maybe you were even some kind of doctor.

"I would go as far as to say perhaps a witch. But you were not the kind associated with the devil, but a benevolent or white witch. I see a clear aura around you along with a wand and a sword. There's also a book to your right, but the contents remain a secret."

Chance suddenly shivered, as if a gust of wind passed through her body.

"Are you alright, Chance?" Alexander asked.

"Yes, I'm fine; but my guides are pulling back for some reason." She decided not to tell Alexander about the horrible image she had seen, an image so disturbing that she was unable to continue.

"I think we should stop here," said Chance, "They've revealed all that they think you should know for now," She whispered.

"Thank you," said Alexander, "It's been wonderful. I'm sure your words will follow me all day."

"I'm sure they will," replied Chance, "It's not often that you learn you might have been a witch in a past life, right?"

She smiled at her first seeker of the day.

"We usually tape the sessions. Once Rhea listens to our reading, she'll leave the tape in your room for you to refer to if you've forgotten any information."

"Only Rhea? Does anyone else get a copy?" Alexander asked, looking a bit worried.

"No my dear, no one else," She answered, "Besides, Rhea already holds the answers and is aware of most of your incarnations. She knew even before your reading. However, like all good lessons learned in a life," Chance emphasized,

"We need to go through the motions, step by step in order to appreciate the enormity of the experience."

As she spoke, Chance cleared off the table, getting ready to enter the next room for her second reading, with Jennifer.

ဆာငလာငလာငလာငလာ

Jennifer

Adriana called Jennifer over to her as soon as the reading had finished. Jennifer left the room looking shocked and rather disoriented.

"Hey Jen, come over here. Tell me what she said!" Adriana screeched, unable to control her enthusiasm.

Adriana was last in line for the reading. Her excitement escalated as each session came to an end.

"Wow, that was amazing," claimed Jennifer, "Adriana, you better prepare yourself for some real time traveling."

"Really? What do you mean? Tell me everything, and the details please, not like the brief summary Alexander gave us. Look at him, he's still walking around in a daze."

"I don't blame him. I feel a little like that myself, a bit disoriented—confusion sprinkled with a touch of fear."

"'Fear of what?'"

"Fear of the unknown. Fear of someone coming into your life, like Chance for example, and reorganizing and changing belief systems that I thought kept me sane."

"That's deep Jen. Now tell me what she said."

Adriana was too eager to hear about Jennifer's reading to occupy her thoughts with philosophical statements.

"Ok, well, she talked a little about my childhood, my parents, specific incidents that no one knows about other than myself. All accurate information, I must add. Then she began addressing my present situation, about studying psychology, friends around me and even about this guy I like from back home."

"Did she ask you any questions?"

"Not at all—she just kept talking as if she were reading my life out of those striking cards. Occasionally she'd ask if what she was saying made sense, just to check if we were on the right track," Jennifer explained.

"Then, she went further back into a previous life."

Adriana listened alertly as Jennifer continued.

"She felt my energy being drawn to Austria, around the late 1800s. I was born into an affluent family. They were involved in different sorts of business and owned a considerable amount of land. Bored and miserable in the confines of my wealthy, respectable Jewish home, I began rebelling against traditions and values upheld by my family for so long."

"Do you remember any of this?" asked Adriana.

"No, not yet, but Chance said the more we concentrate on the details, the more likely we are to perhaps trigger something that will allow us to tap into the memory of our previous lives."

"Go on," Urged Adriana, "This is so interesting."

"Where was I? Yes, about rebelling and getting into all kinds of trouble. Apparently, after my mother's death, I developed some kind of 'hysteria,' as they called it back then. Basically, I went crazy; Chance kept talking about my struggle with madness and trying to remain sane."

"Chance said she saw me surrounded by supportive people, including one man who tried to cure me of my illness. I was in a therapeutic environment for many years, including various mental institutes and sanatoriums. She even wrote down the name of one of the hospitals."

Jennifer reached into her pocket and took out a folded piece of paper.

"Look, it was called Bellevue Sanatorium at Kreuzlingen."

Jennifer held the piece of paper with as much care as she would her birth certificate.

"Go on," Adriana said.

"Well, apparently it's that man, perhaps my psychiatrist, that I need to think about."

"The one who tried to cure you of your hysteria?"

"Yes, the connection to him seems to be imperative in discovering what went wrong and why I have this unexplainable desire to return to Austria."

"So, Chance couldn't tell you more about that?"

"No, she said Dameer's role in this process would unravel the rest of the story."

"Amazing! Where's Daniel? He's supposed to go in next."

"I think he already has," Jennifer said, wondering if Daniel would be as bewildered as she and Alexander had been.

ဆာလ္ဆာလ္ဆာလ္ဆာလ္

Daniel

(Journal Entry 2)

I thought writing the first journal entry was hard; man this is going to be tougher! I'm not sure if I remember all the details, but anyway, here I go. Chance seems like a very nice lady, kind of special. I felt pretty comfortable with her as soon as I sat down. She didn't waste much time chit chatting; we got down to the reading right away.

I'm not sure if I'm supposed to explain all the details of how the reading was done. I'm sure you all know about her methods and stuff, so I'll just summarize that part. While shuffling her cards, I was asked to think deeply about my troubles and any specific question I have. I concentrated real hard, especially while picking 12 cards out of the deck, which she laid out in front of us in the shape of a tree.

It's so funny how she talks to herself and the cards. Each card seemed to tell her something, to reveal a secret to her. At one point, I thought maybe she has some invisible friends like I have!

Anyway, she started out by giving me a little background about my life. She described my past like I would tell one of my friends about a movie I saw, with so much accuracy and detail. I have to be honest with you, that part freaked me out a bit because I've never been to a psychic before. She talked about my insecurities, lack of confidence, not being able to really make or keep friends for too long because of my anger and bitterness towards everything. But what really surprised me was the stuff about my mom. She could feel her pain and said that she was constantly worried about me. I know that's true, and I feel so guilty about it. Dr Hartley says I shouldn't feel guilty; it's just another negative emotion that will stand in the way of my "therapeutic progression." FUCK DOCTOR HARTLEY AND HIS THERAPUTIC PROGRESSION! I'm sorry about my language, but it's just that he doesn't get it sometimes, actually most of the time. I mean, that's my mom. How could I feel good about what I've done to her?

Anyway, I shuffled the cards another time so we could look at one of my other lives, as Chance told me to do. Here's where things get really freaky. Apparently, I was some kind of doctor in the life that seems to be causing problems in this life, and not your regular family doctor. Are you ready for this? I was a fucking shrink! She said I was born sometime in the mid 1800s in France. I worked as a physician at an asylum set up for the mentally ill that was in the countryside just outside of Paris. Chance talked about the cramped and dirty conditions the patients were kept in. She said I was insensitive in a way and heavily into my work. At one point she almost started crying, saying she felt so bad for the people there, that she was horrified at the way they were being treated.

I couldn't really relate to why she suddenly broke down like that. Maybe it was the images she saw or the stuff the cards showed. We ended there and Chance asked me to think about what we'd talked about.

I don't know what to think or feel about my reading. I didn't really know what to expect, so anything she said would have come as a surprise, especially since I don't know much about reincarnation or past lives. But how incredibly ironic for me to have been a type of psychiatrist, considering how I feel about them in this life. Or do I hate them so much because I was one myself previously, and deep down inside, somewhere in my heart of hearts, I know what they're capable of? See, she's got me thinking already! That explains my extreme dislike towards psychotherapists, but what about my condition? I asked Chance how that might be related, and she said Dameer would be the one to take me further through these revelations about my past lives and how they relate to my present.

So I guess we're half way there. I have to admit this has been a crazy experience for me. You guys are cool, and it's so nice to find people who genuinely care about others without wanting anything in return. I had almost lost hope in humanity, thinking that we'd evolved into a bunch of selfish humans, preoccupied only with our own stuff. Maybe I've been too critical. Maybe I need to learn from you guys and give a little myself.

ಬಿ)(ಐ ಬಿ)(ಐ ಬಿ)(ಐ ಬಿ)(ಐ

Adriana

Rhea sat back in her chair, thinking about the readings she had been listening to. Once again, Chance had pinpointed the past life that was causing conflict in each of her guests' present lives beautifully. She wondered about all the souls that had touched her and Chance's life while working at the Karma Hotel. She often thought about the ones that had had the most impact on her.

After a difficult incident, she had decided not to keep in touch with former guests any longer. This particular young man was quite taken by Rhea, sending her letters almost every week. He requested that he be allowed to come back to the hotel but was politely rejected repeatedly due to the rules and regulations upheld by the establishment. The Council believed each person should be allowed to enter this center of enlightenment only once. This way others could be offered an opportunity to visit The Karma Hotel. The person in question had become obsessed with Rhea and her work and was unable to detach from his experience there. Eventually, he understood that he must let go of a dangerous fantasy and live a more realistic existence.

She still thought about, even worried about that young man. Daniel reminded her a bit of him. That's why she was especially intrigued by his history and reaction to Chance's reading. She wondered how he would perceive the rest of the story, as Dameer worked on bringing the details further to the surface.

Rhea decided to shift her attention to Adriana. She had listened to her reading once but wanted to hear it again. She took Daniel's recording out of the tape player and inserted the tape on which Adriana's session had been recorded. Rhea poured some water in her glass, sat forward in her chair and pressed the play button.

"Hi Adriana, please have a seat."

"Hi, you must be tired after doing three other readings, right?"

"Intrigued, yes. Tired, never. I use a technique to restore my energy after each reading. It helps to rebalance my mind. Nevertheless, I try not to do more than four readings a day. Not because I get tired but to ensure accuracy for my seekers. We wouldn't want my guides to get all confused now, would we?"

"Ummm, I guess not."

"Enough about me. Let's begin. I want you to hold these cards as if you were holding a sacred treasure. Let your entire essence be felt by them. While holding the cards, think about problems or obstacles that may be hindering your spiritual or physical progression. You may also ask specific questions if you wish."

"Alright," said Adriana and then there was a pause.

"Now pick 12 cards with your left hand and pass them to me, one by one."

"From anywhere in the pile?"

"Yes, think about the reason for choosing a particular card. Allow yourself to be drawn to them." There was another pause on the tape.

"Thank you. Adriana. You're quite a skeptic, aren't you? It's not that you think I'm a phony, but you're not sure whether to believe or accept what I tell you. That's all right. I like seekers such as yourself. It's more of a challenge to impress you!"

"It's not that I don't believe in your powers Chance. I've just never been one to depend on the abstract. I guess I'm too pragmatic for this stuff."

"No need to explain. We're all different from one another, in our beliefs, values and opinions, and that's what makes each of us unique. However, there are certain commonalities that we forget about, such as the words of the heart. The heart never lies. It may hide or avoid a question, but it is incapable of altering the truth. I'll be speaking to your heart today and then we'll decide whether your pragmatic nature will win over the most important part of your body."

"I like the way you explain things. It makes more sense to me now."

"You've had a very content and comfortable life. You're quite level-headed and never got into any kind of trouble as a teenager, am I right?"

"Ahha."

"This can be partly attributed to your stable home life and the way you were raised by your mother and father. But also, these facts are very much part of your nature and character.

"You are cautious yet never settle for the status quo, always striving to do better and reach higher aspirations. This is particularly true in regards to your occupation. Keep up the great work; you're highly respected by your peers and supervisors. I would even go as far as to say that one day you may become a partner within the company you're working for."

"Wow, that's great to know."

"You are kind, but not gullible. You've been there for friends on many occasions, but at the same time, have turned your back on those who have done you wrong, never regretting your decision to disconnect or let go of negative friendships.

"You seem to be an older soul, not quite what I'd call advanced but definitely at an intermediate level. That's why you seem to have a healthy grasp of what life's all about. You're quite modest about your achievements and don't let obstacles stifle your progression. Does all this make sense to you?"

"Yes, completely."

"You've reached a level where you are comfortable with who you are and your position in this life. You're open to others, not afraid to let them in emotionally, or afraid of losing them eventually.

"In other words, you're more trusting than suspicious of people, which makes you more of an optimist. This attitude of faith and confidence in the people around you is highly attractive, drawing people towards you."

"Ahha."

"Ahhhh, here's where lessons need to be learned. I can see you haven't been very lucky with men. They seem to come and go a lot. Some have stayed longer than others, but generally your romances seem to die out as soon as they begin. Is that right?"

"Yes, very true. Why is that? I mean, I think I work really hard at my relationships, but somehow I always hit a dead end."

"Of course with every relationship there are various factors and forces either making it or breaking it. But generally failure is due to two reasons: partly because you will not settle for anything less than what you think you deserve, so as soon as a man has not lived up to your expectations you're ready to walk, and also due to the way you have dealt with relationships in your past lives.

"There are some unresolved or unconsummated love affairs that need to be addressed. Whose name starts with an 'S'?"

"The man I'm in love with is named Stephen,"

"And what a special man he is. He loves you dearly, Adriana."

There is now a long pause on the tape.

"Please pick four more cards from the deck with your right hand."

"Ok."

"Hmmmm, this is where the problem lies. I thought this was too good to be true. He's married, isn't he?"

"Yes."

"I don't know if this will make you feel any better, but he's not happy with his partner. It's not for any particular reason. It's just that their energies are in total disharmony. They aren't made for each other, not in this life or any other to follow."

"So, why won't he leave her?"

"Let's ask the cards! Pick six more cards from the deck please."

There is another long pause and the sound of the cards being laid upon the table.

"We would need to dive into your past incarnations to get a clearer picture of what is going on, but the cards seem to think it has something to do with his nature. He would rather sacrifice his own happiness for the sake of his family and children. He feels he's obligated to them morally."

"That definitely sounds like Stephen."

"All right, now let's move back to that life that seems to be hindering your relationship with Stephen. Please shuffle the cards once again while focusing on your man. Pick out 21 cards with your right hand. I always ask my seekers to concentrate on the details I'll be exposing; I'd like you to do the same.

"However odd it may seem, try to picture yourself as the main character of that narrative. Think back to any dreams or flashbacks you may have had in your life related to our reading."

"Ok, I'll try my best." There is only the sound of cards being handled.

"This is interesting. I feel like we're going way back in time. Around the 11th century in ancient Persia. You were a man in this life, and a very powerful one, both in terms of political position and wealth. You are a very prominent member of that society surrounded by opulence and luxury."

"How do you know that, Chance?"

"The cards and my guides are telling me. Don't try to rationalize these facts my dear. A few hundred years from now you may receive a similar reading regarding your present life as 'Adriana.'

"It's that simple. While we're on the topic, let me share a beautiful quote from a Persian poet called Rumi. He said 'Knowing too much hinders knowing at all. And thought brings no comprehension.'"

"Wow, that's deep. Can I have a few lifetimes to think about it?"

"You're too modest Adriana. I'm sure you've already deciphered the messages behind the statement. Now, where were we? Yes, you were very popular, yet so lonely. You were surrounded by hundreds of people yet aching only for one.

"Even in this life, you were unlucky in love. You seemed to be very mistrusting of women who crossed your path, always worried that they may not love you for 'you' but more for your position of power and wealth. So who's this person that finally won your heart? Please pick three more cards with your right hand."

"Could Stephen have been incarnated as a woman in that life?"

"Let's see. I wouldn't be able to say exactly unless I were to do a reading with him present. However, we can try. Repeat his full name and hold his image in your thoughts while choosing the cards."

"Ok."

"I see a woman from a different class both socially and financially than the one to which you belong—a very beautiful woman whom you fell head over heals in love with. You met coincidentally. I don't think she ever knew about your wealth or your true identity.

"Now, I don't mean that you deceived her, but somehow she fell equally in love for no other reason than the person you portrayed to her, exactly as you had always dreamed. Adriana, I sense a beautiful love story, embodying both sweet and bitter times."

"Did we ever marry?"

"No, this affair seems to be shrouded with secrecy, an unconsummated love. I think it might have been Stephen, just because of the way this story seems so similar to one you're experiencing with him in this life. I sense so much pain and fear, so much interference from other people, especially family members.

"Chance, are you alright?"

"Yes, I'm fine my dear. In order to recount the tale I often get too involved in the story, sensing every emotion that my seekers felt. I'll be fine. It seems that my guides have pulled back."

"Does that mean we can't continue? That you can't tell me what happened between this woman and me so many years ago? I mean Stephen and me? I mean … well, you know what I mean!"

"Yes Adriana. We must stop here. Please think carefully about our discussion today. Concentrate on little details that may trigger buried memories. Dameer will help shed more light on this beautiful love story. I wish you all the luck in the world. Never give up on love."

"Thank you, Chance. This has been quite an experience. Jennifer was right to prepare me for quite an emotional roller coaster."

"You're welcome, my dear. Now I advise you to rest a little before we meet for dinner. Perhaps take this time to write about our session in your diary."

"Good idea. I'll do that. See you later."

Rhea stopped the tape. She was pleased that Chance had not dived so deeply into Adriana's story. She had appropriately opened the door to Adriana's past incarnation. Emotionally, her guests were in quite a vulnerable position. Divulging too much information may shock them, or worse yet, leave them feeling quite raw, especially because the session must inevitably end without having an opportunity to examine the seeker's feelings about what they've heard. There was no doubt regarding Chance's ability; nevertheless, she was incapable of providing both a reading and a counseling session. The opened wounds would need to be treated with utmost care to avoid emotional infections. Chance would leave that part of the healing to Latifah and Dameer.

ഇരുള

Latifah

"*He saw that there was no mood of the mind that had not its counterpart in the sensuous life, and set himself to discover their true relations, wondering what there was in frankincense that made one mystical, and in ambergris that stirred one's passions, and violets that woke the memory of dead romances and in musk that troubled the brain ...*"

—Oscar Wilde (*The Picture of Dorian Gray*)

Latifah woke up early in order to prepare for the day ahead. She was familiar with Jennifer, Alexander, Daniel and Adriana, but not familiar enough to make any assumptions pertaining to their condition or progression. Nevertheless, she knew they would enjoy some pampering after being on adventures with Magic and Chance. Especially after their time with Chance—because Chance had opened the door to each one's past, and perhaps to the abstruse causes of their affliction. *No amount of preparation can protect a person from finding out about a past life. It can be quite disturbing for some, if not life altering.* That is why Rhea exposed the truth in stages. This way her guests had an opportunity to digest the incredible events unfolding before them.

Latifah's role complimented Chance's readings beautifully. Latifah stepped in to give each guest an exceptional massage the day after their specific encounters with 'the past'. She started off by preparing special room sprays, using different oils and scents—to meet the needs of each person accordingly. The main function of this heavenly concoction would be to help them sleep better. Chance would have definitely hit sensitive and emotional points in each of the clients; therefore it would not be surprising if they were unable to rest, replaying Chance's words in their thoughts.

The night before, she entered each of their rooms while the seekers ate dinner with Chance, Dameer, Rhea and Adam, generously spraying the surroundings, especially the bed, with her unique blend of resting potion. Other than promising relaxation, the resting potion also brought with it more vivid and colorful dreams, the kind that stay with us for a lifetime, visiting us from time to time.

Latifah felt confident that her clients would have had a very tranquil and restful night. This knowledge stemmed from previous guests who would awaken after experiencing her rest potion—all of whom claimed to feel rejuvenated, almost reborn. They would hug her and cry, explaining how they had tried all kinds of other treatments, from sleeping pills to various herbal remedies, all failing miserably. She could sense and see the immediate effects of deep relaxation expressed all over their aura. Did they look younger? *Perhaps the powers of a good night's sleep, my reader, are priceless.*

Latifah prepared her oils for mixing, creating four special blends. She was quite proud of her high quality oils that made the massage even more special. Not only would the essential oils increase the oxygenation to the cells, but they also possessed an aroma that lingered with the senses for days, following the mind and soul to ensure lengthened relaxation. Her treatment of the guests would be the perfect prelude to their encounter with Dameer.

Latifah's main objective was to rebalance her client's energy levels through a deep massage, working her way along the major muscles and pressure points throughout the body. She started by rubbing the neck and shoulders and the upper back, then gradually covered the rest of the body through a deep treatment involving pushing, squeezing and kneading the skin. At first, most people were surprised at her strength and would express discomfort. She would only lessen her force in rare circumstances, however, if the person were infirm or especially vociferous in their complaints. She needed to get deep, to reach points that ached for her magic touch.

She thought back to the different reactions people have during a session. Some fall asleep; others discuss world events or private matters, while other people get completely flooded by the release of tension jailed within their bodies. The emotional roller coaster that accompanies a session of aromatherapy and massage usually encompasses both sad and happy emotions, and sometimes an uncomfortable combination of the two. She remembered one particular client who used up her entire session crying. Latifah never once interrupted her stream of tears. She let her feel. She let her experience the release of sadness.

Dear reader, why must we keep such anger and pain closed up inside our hearts? Why must we poison our system with emotions that can only pollute our minds? Perhaps we should spend less time thinking about environmental issues and focus more on the internal destruction and massacre that we ruthlessly engage in on a daily basis. Only then can we begin to understand the unnecessary damage we inflict on nature.

After preparing the final touches, Latifah headed for Rhea's office. Rhea usually briefed Latifah about each client's progression and any special concerns that she might have about the guests just before Latifah met with them. Latifah was eager to start, knowing that with each new client, a lesson was waiting to be learned.

ഇ൫ഇ൫ഇ൫ഇ൫

The Gathering

"There's Adriana, look at her gliding her way towards us!" Daniel said as he looked towards the therapy room.

The guests had all decided to meet after their session with Latifah, and Adriana was last to finish. Somehow, their experience during the last few days had brought them very close. They found themselves spending more and more time with each other.

Who would have thought Daniel would put an ounce of effort into any kind of relationship, let alone open his heart to bonding with three strangers? Certainly not Daniel, for he was as shocked to realize he thought about and missed Adriana, Jennifer and Alexander when away from them. He actually thought before speaking and was conscious about saying nice things. Suddenly, trying to make a favorable impression on others was not such a terrible and impossible task. Daniel regretted putting so much negative energy into making people not like him. 'What a waste of time—and lost relationships,' He thought.

"Is Latifah incredible or what?" sighed Adriana, sounding intoxicated.

"I know. She's out of this world! We've just been sitting here discussing each of our experiences with her. I don't want to talk too much in fear of losing this heavenly feeling," said Alexander.

"Well, you're just going to have to repeat yourself because I'd love to know how you all felt throughout your sessions," Adriana said.

"She's definitely got the magic touch. Half of the time I didn't know if I was sleeping or awake," said Jennifer.

"You think she slipped some drugs or something into those oils she uses? Man, I tell you, I still feel kind of high!" Daniel added.

"I don't know but whatever she used, it was out of this world," Jennifer explained, "Suddenly, I found myself sighing with pleasure, repeatedly. Then I started to cry, for no particular reason."

In truth, Jennifer had cried for many reasons, but some she chose to keep private.

"I did too Jen. I laughed and cried and then laughed some more. All kinds of thoughts invaded my mind. Some happy, others a little bit more heart tugging," Alexander said.

"I had various thoughts during the session as well, and I expressed them to her," said Adriana, "She didn't really agree or disagree. She just listened and continued massaging. I felt the need to talk—especially because she told me to think about what Chance had said. At one point I must have drifted off into a sleep state. I started dreaming about my past life. Did that happen to you guys?"

They all nodded in agreement, confirming a similar experience. Daniel spoke about the images of an asylum that had played in his mind. Jennifer talked about her life in Austria, about feelings of desperation and lost hope, but she said that she was still not too sure about the details of her deep pain. Alexander felt empowered thinking about being a witch and surrounded by magic spells and powerful amulets. How wonderful to be able to help people through supernatural methods. 'So what had gone wrong?' He thought.

It was Adriana who seemed to have the most intense experience during her session with Latifah. She talked about feeling in touch with her masculine side as she thought about being a rich and powerful man in that life. At one point, Adriana imagined her lover caressing her. Suddenly, she was transported back in time. Latifah was replaced by a gorgeous young woman whispering words of passion and eating every inch of her male body with her hands.

Adriana was reminded of the way Stephen massaged her—the way he covered every corner, every curve of her silky smooth skin. He would arrange everything: the candles, the rose pedals scattered around the room, the soft music, and the peach scented oil he would use for her trip to heaven. She said that her mind switched from one scene, one time to another in a matter of seconds. Until finally, worried that she may be having a nightmare, Latifah awakened Adriana. Adriana was drenched in sweat and confused about her surroundings. Latifah carefully explained what had happened, wiped her body of the toxins she had released during her time travel and asked her to try and relax once again.

The others listened carefully as Adriana told her story. Her experience only fueled their excitement, their hunger to learn more about the particular life that was causing problems in their present existence. However, they would have to wait until later on that afternoon for their meeting with Dameer. Now they had lunch to think about. Adam had prepared yet another delectable and taste bud teasing melody of dishes. They slowly got up from their resting area and walked towards the dining hall where Rhea stood waiting for them.

ଅଚ୍ଛଅଚ୍ଛଅଚ୍ଛଅଚ୍ଛ

Dameer

"It is the secret of the world that all things subsist and do not die, but only retire a little from sight and afterwards return again. Nothing is dead; men feign themselves dead, and endure mock funerals and mournful obituaries, and there they stand looking out of the window, sound and well, in some new strange disguise."

—Ralph Waldo Emerson (*Essays, Series 2*)

"I just spoke to Latifah and she was very pleased with each of your sessions," Rhea said after all had finished eating a light lunch.

"I think we were equally pleased!" Expressed Alexander, from the depths of his heart.

The rest of the group nodded in agreement and said similar words of gratitude. They all felt quite relaxed. Daniel talked about how 'airy' he felt, almost as if he were floating rather than walking. The effect of Latifah's enchanting massage was still very much felt by everyone who had experienced it.

"You're very welcome. I'm so glad that you're enjoying your stay with us. Now it's time for the most important, or perhaps enlightening, part of your therapy." As Rhea began talking about the next phase, she looked towards Dameer and smiled because he would play an integral role.

"It's essential that we conduct this part of your rehabilitation today, when you're feeling relaxed after your meeting with Latifah. I'll let Dameer explain the rest of it to you." Rhea shifted her full attention towards Dameer, signaling him to address their guests.

"That's right Rhea, we should begin almost immediately. Let me tell you why. The next stage of our program involves a session of hypnosis, which is one of the most common ways of exploring past lives.

"Through hypnosis, we can tap into and hopefully activate the subconscious mind. It is in this part of our thoughts that certain past life memories may be stored, and the more relaxed you are, the more able you will be to open to those deeper levels of your subconscious," Dameer said.

"Hey Doc, I hope you're not going to make us bark like dogs and take off our clothes! I've seen people under hypnosis doing some strange things on TV," Daniel said, making the others laugh.

"I've seen those images too Daniel, but what we're going to do will be quite different. We have a concrete purpose, and that is to try to gain a better understanding of what might have occurred during that past life that Chance has already spoken to each of you about.

"No one can provide as detailed an insight as the seeker, which is of course you. And I assure you, I won't turn any of you into dogs or any other kinds of animals!" Dameer said laughing, trying to ease his clients' anxiety.

"So how does it work, Dameer? Is hypnosis a kind of sleep state? Will we know what's going on around us?" asked Adriana, worried about the potential loss of control and consciousness that hypnosis might encompass.

"You see, I want you to think about hypnosis as a kind of deep meditation. You will be completely aware of your surroundings, of my voice and presence. It's like a trance state that blocks out all the distractions that inhibit this secret part of our mind.

"You cannot be made to do or say anything that you don't wish to do or say. You will be the driver throughout this adventure. I merely act as the vehicle that aids in making the exploration occur," explained Dameer.

Of all the members of the group, perhaps Jennifer knew most about this altered state of consciousness. She had studied it in her Introduction to Psychology class. Her instructor had brought in a guest speaker to demonstrate how it worked. She had been fascinated by its powers, especially after viewing a documentary of a woman who was allergic to anesthetics and had a cesarean while under hypnosis to block the pain of surgery. She recalled the way the mother-to-be sang 'We are the World' right through her operation!

"Each person has a different experience of past life regression," Dameer continued, "Some see the past life as if they were watching a movie, quite detached both from emotions and the event.

"Others, on the other hand, may actually relive the experience in its full intensity. However, regardless of the type of experience each of you have, the important part of this exercise is to try to remain focused and open to the details that unfold before us," Dameer said.

"How many sessions will we have, Dameer, and where will they take place?" asked Jennifer, who was eager to see if she was able to be hypnotized.

Jennifer's lecturer had informed them that only a very small percentage of the population should not be guided into this type of deep relaxed state.

"There will be one main session, but it will depend on the way in which we progress. Some of you may need more coaxing if the initial sessions don't bring about the desired outcome. However, our guests usually cope quite well with our method and find the answers to their concerns within one meeting."

Dameer studied the guests' faces for signs of confusion. Fortunately, they seemed more curious than anything.

"I think Daniel might need more than a couple of sessions!" teased Jennifer, putting her arm around Daniel.

"Well, let's see what happens. You might be very surprised," said Dameer.

"Is there a special room for each of our sessions?" asked Alexander.

"No, we won't be meeting in rooms. Remember the hammocks in the lobby?"

Together, the guests all nodded.

"I'm not sure if Rhea or Arya told you about the special therapeutic powers those hammocks have," continued Dameer, "but they aren't just any old swinging devices."

Dameer looked over at Rhea and smiled. She returned his smile with a wink of secret understanding.

"We use them for you to lie on during the process of hypnosis. Now I think we should make our way towards the lobby to turn some of this theoretical information into an experiential operation."

Dameer picked up his briefcase and what looked like a small folding chair and asked the seekers to follow him towards the lobby.

Rhea watched them walk out of the dining hall. She felt an indescribably deep commitment and attachment towards these people affected by problems of different causes and intensity. There were millions more like them out in the, sometimes cold and lonely, world. She planned to reach as many of those individuals as she possibly could.

After all, my spiritual thinker, what kind of life is one without a purpose? What kind of existence does someone have without being able to give and to make a difference in other people's lives? A life without service to others was definitely not the kind of reality One wanted to be part of. Next time the universe invites you to impress her through an act of generosity, accept the offer with a smile, my dear. The rewards will be immeasurable.

ഇരുജ്ഞരുജ്ഞരുജ്ഞരുജ്ഞ

The Hammocks …

After arriving in the lobby, Dameer instructed each of his guests to lie on a hammock. There were four different ones, each distinctively decorated in terms of color and pattern. The hammocks were positioned a few meters apart from one another. Jennifer, Daniel, Alexander and Adriana walked towards the closest hammock to them and lay down.

"Now, for the initial phase, I'll be speaking to you simultaneously. I want you to relax, close your eyes and saturate yourself with the feeling of serenity. Once we've established that, an enclosure will rise around your hammock, separating you from each other. Let me show you before we begin."

Dameer stepped away from the rest of the group and towards a podium covered by flowers and ivy. He gently pushed the greenery aside, inspected the different levers, and proceeded to press on various buttons.

Suddenly, glass enclosures began rising out from the lobby floor, surrounding each hammock. Alexander felt relieved about it not being too small or suffocating, which would definitely distract him from feeling relaxed. The glass cage looked almost invisible so the guests would not feel uncomfortable or claustrophobic in any way. There was a door on one side of the enclosure. Alexander wondered if it was meant for people who wanted to walk out in the middle of the session. He chose not to ask Dameer, and instead decided to wait for an explanation before letting his anxiety take over his imagination.

Dameer pressed the buttons again and the glass walls disappeared smoothly into the floor.

"Once the glass enclosure is up, and you've achieved a deep state of meditation, I'll join you individually, in your separate cells, to begin the individual process."

'Ahhh, that's what the door is for', thought Alexander.

"You'll be asked to think about various questions and scenarios. Please take your time and reflect on the images that my questions elicit. Try to provide as detailed an answer as you can because more information will lead to more insight."

"Will the others hear our answers?" asked Daniel.

"No, that's precisely why we have the glass enclosure. Your answers will automatically be recorded through our sound system attached to each hammock. Only Rhea and I will have access to the information."

"What will the rest of us be doing while you're with Alexander, for example?" wondered Adriana aloud.

Adriana was not too sure she could maintain this trance state for very long. She immediately thought about how Yoga classes bored the hell out of her.

"Adriana, time and space will be greatly altered during this procedure. It won't feel like you're sitting in a waiting room of a doctor's office, I assure you. Quite the contrary, most people wish they could remain in that deep state of relaxation for as long as possible without being disturbed. Trust me, lengthy instructions and explanations kill the magic of hypnosis, let's dive in! Any other questions?"

They all shook their head, eager to maintain the enchantment.

"All right, we're ready to begin." Dameer took a deep breath, unfolded his chair and sat in between the hammocks. "I want you to move around on the hammock until you're in a comfortable position. Close your eyes, ignoring any sounds other than my voice. Take a few deep breaths, deeper than you've taken a breath ever before. As you inhale and exhale, think about the word 'relaxation'."

Dameer stopped for a moment, allowing them to get comfortable and aquatinted with the meditation.

"As you're breathing in and out, allow this new kind of relaxation to take over your entire body, starting from your head and moving downward to your feet. Breathe in tranquility and breathe out any stress that may be trapped within each pore." He continued soothing their minds with similar words, speaking softly yet in quite a directive manner.

"I will count backwards from ten to one, and by the time I reach one, you'll feel completely relaxed. You'll think about what I'm saying, but my words will not distract you.

"They will only guide you into the unexplored areas of your mind. You're feeling more and more relaxed and getting drowsier by the second. You've discarded all the stress and tension of everyday life, and the only thing you care about is trying to sink deeper into this heavenly feeling."

While counting backward, Dameer watched the four individuals slipping into a blissful mood. Calm and serenity invaded every atom of their physical state. Watching this transformation always amazed him, even after having witnessed it over and over during the last twenty years of his career. Their bodies were lying still. Dameer paused for a few seconds to allow them to sink deeper.

"You are completely relaxed in every way. My voice further relaxes you as I ask you to think about certain scenes in your mind. Imagine yourself as a part of a summer sky ... you seem so light and airy ... watching the clouds floating by. See yourself flying effortlessly ...

"You become even more relaxed as you soar through the sky. Imagine yourself flying backward now ... not only backward in direction, but also in time. As you do this, picture yourself getting younger and younger ... your image changing with every age that you regress to." Dameer paused again, allowing time for reflection.

"The further you reach into your youth, the more relaxed you feel. As the image changes, you are fully aware that you're looking at phases in your life that have molded your present personality, made you into who you are today."

This was the most crucial part of the hypnosis.

"The image blurs for a moment, and this change sinks you even deeper. Imagine a new image forming. It may seem vague at first, but then it begins to sharpen. You may not think that the person is you, because you see a different picture of yourself.

"Think about moving your hand or legs. You'll see as you move, the image mimics the movements you make. You notice that even though the person you see may not look like you in this life, it is you from another life. More specifically, it is you from the life that has the greatest significance to your concerns or unanswered questions in your present existence."

Dameer paused again, allowing them to get familiar with their new 'selves.' He quietly rose from his seat, grabbed his chair, walked towards the podium and pressed the appropriate buttons in order to activate the glass enclosures.

ℰℭ𝔅ℭℰℭℛℭℰℭℛℭ

Alexander

Dameer walked towards Alexander's hammock and opened the glass door to his enclosure, remaining as unobtrusive as he possibly could. They were all in a deep state of relaxation and would take no notice of outside noise; nevertheless he did not want to distract them even a little from their journey. He sat down and began the exploration we've all been waiting for. ***Wasn't it worth the wait? Who ever said 'patience is a virtue' was right, because the universe's delays should never be mistaken for her denials.***

"I want you to think about that impression that has formed before you. Look at the reflection and concentrate on the details you see. See it, feel it, relate to it and trust that this person is you from a past life. I'll ask you questions regarding that image so please take your time when answering."

Dameer Continued, "Do you see a male or female image?"

"I'm a female. Not very attractive, but a kind woman. I'm wearing a long black robe. It's old but comfortable. I have long black hair, with gray streaks," Alexander answered dreamily.

"Do you know your name and what year it is?"

"Elisabeth … I don't know the date exactly, but I think it's around 1653. I live in a village in England. There are a lot of poor people around. I'm one of them. But there are some rich people who control everything. They live a good life."

"What are your surroundings like?"

"I'm in my house, and I love it here. I seek refuge in my home when the outside world gets to be too much."

"What do you mean by too much'?" inquired Dameer.

"People don't like me. They are afraid of me because they know about my powers."

"What powers?"

"I'm a healer … they call me a witch and other things. It hurts me … I hear all the names they call me behind my back. They are so mean," whispered Alexander.

"What do you mean by healer?"

"I have a gift. I've been given special powers to help those in need. They come to me with their problems and I cure them."

"How?"

"Through magic spells, herbs and spices, different types of drinks and food. Sometimes, instead of those in need coming to me, I find them. I can read their thoughts … I know they are hurting. It doesn't make people feel very comfortable when I do that. But their fear usually eases once they know I mean no harm."

"What kind of problems do these people have?"

"It can be anything … having problems with a husband or wife … not smelling good … being shy or lacking confidence … stomach pains … general bad health. I've seen all sorts of troubles," he answered simply.

"How do you feel right now? Are you happy?"

"I feel most fulfilled after helping someone, but most of the time I'm lonely. People around here don't accept me because I never married. I'm a threat to their way of life and to their ideas of what is acceptable and what is strange. But they need me and always come back."

"Let's move forward in time. Think about the point during this life that you feel most sad about. What happened?"

Alexander took a deep breath then answered quickly.

"She turned on me, a very vindictive and evil woman. I hate her. She makes me suffer so badly."

"Who is she?"

"Her name is Katherine."

"Is she someone you know in your current life?"

Alexander paused for a while.

"Yes, I do."

"Who is she?" Asked Dameer.

"Daniel."

Dameer made a quick note of this revelation. It's not uncommon at all to recognize people in our present lives who had an impact on one of our past lives. This knowledge would be paramount in the healing process.

"What happened between you?" Dameer watched Alexander as he squirmed uncomfortably on the hammock. He allowed him to think, without interruption.

"She asked me to put a spell on the man she loves. He doesn't love her, you see. He doesn't want her. But Katherine can't accept that. I tell her I don't cast such spells. The affairs of the heart are very sensitive and should never be tampered with. The consequences can be dire. No heart can be forced into loving."

"How was she vindictive?" Dameer searched for more detail.

"She keeps coming back … she's so desperate … acts like a mad woman … keeps threatening me."

Alexander's breathing started to get heavier.

"How does she threaten you?"

"She says that she'll tell the officials that I'm a witch, an evil woman who does not behave morally. She's from a privileged family, and I fear they will believe her. Why the hell should anyone believe an ugly old woman?"

"Did she tell them?"

"Yes."

"Did they believe her?"

"Yes."

"Tell me what happened."

"She spread all kinds of lies about me to everyone in the village, turned them all against me. People can be so cruel. They don't realize the damage a loose tongue can cause. Words can break a person's soul. She spread such nasty lies about me."

"Do you remember what they were saying?"

"That I'm a flesh eating witch, that I kill babies and infants, cut them up in pieces and use their organs for ingredients in magic spells. That I'm after their husbands, after men they want. They don't know the weight of their words. They don't know how evil gossip can be."

Seeing Alexander getting worked up, Dameer decided to detach him from that time and move a little forward.

"Take me further. Tell me what happened as a result of this gossip."

"The officials and some of the other women from the village, including Katharine, stormed into my house one night, pulled me out of bed and beat me badly. They kicked me in the stomach, dragged me out of my home by my hair and beat me some more. It hurts terribly … it's so unfair."

"If you're feeling uncomfortable, try to separate yourself from these. Float above the scene and describe it as if watching a movie."

Alexander continued, ignoring Dameer's comment.

"They took me to a dungeon … I don't know where it is. I'm blindfolded and my hands are tied. It's so dark and cold, and I haven't eaten for days. I know what's awaiting me. I know what they do to women suspected to be witches."

"What did they do to you?"

"They kept me there for some time. I'm not sure how long, maybe a few weeks, but it feels like an eternity. At times I am cramped and stiff from sitting in the same position and can hardly move for the pain. The utter darkness behind the blindfold scares me to death, and I'm sure every sound is men coming to get me, to take me to what awaits me.

"It is horrible, just horrible. Finally someone does come to take me out of my cell. I'm still blindfolded and can see nothing, but by the sounds I know that he has taken me out into the town center. I can hear people jeering at me, laughing and throwing things as I walk."

"Go on."

"I'm walking up a set of stairs, and he's pushing me forward. He's ruthless, completely without mercy. His intense grip is draining the blood away from my arm. I want to die. I want the pain and fear to end. I've suffered so badly."

"Did they hang you?"

"No. That would have been too quick an end, too easy a death. They want revenge; they want me to suffer."

"What happened next?"

"I feel stones hitting my body from all directions and they are like daggers into my soul. The pain seems endless, and I beg God to let me die. Just when I think I can't breathe anymore and I see death's face staring at me, I sense the heat of the flame coming towards me."

Alexander's breathing was very heavy now.

"They all laughed as I burned in front of the whole village. So many people watching, and I had helped most of them. This is how they repay me … I'm in so much pain!"

Alexander cried uncontrollably, but soon his breathing slowed down allowing his facial muscles to relax and the tears to slow. He put his head back into a resting position and took a few deep breaths.

"How do you think your periods of fatigue may relate to events of that time?" Dameer asked, looking for a specific answer.

"I'm not quite sure … maybe all these lifetimes I've carried the pain I felt while in solitary confinement. Maybe my periods of darkness in this life are a result of being punished unjustly in my life as a healer, which I have taken as a sign from the universe to be cautious about who I help."

"Very good. Tell me what else you're thinking about Alex?"

"I'm thinking about pain and injustice. I didn't deserve to be treated that way."

"Yes, you're right. You didn't. I want you to meditate on that experience and think about other relevant lessons that you learned. I'll count backward from five to one and you'll slowly float away from those images."

"I want you to try to forgive, maybe even begin to feel love for those who hurt you. Focus on love and forgiveness."

Dameer stood up quietly, grabbed his folding chair and walked out of the glass cell. The smile on Alexander's face was a definite sign that he was beginning to release his soul of the bitterness, resentment and fear he had carried with him since that life as a healer. He was ready to embrace love and forgiveness.

ഇരുളില്‍

Jennifer

Dameer walked into Jennifer's glass enclosure and quietly sat down. She looked so peaceful—miles away. She was obviously in a deep tranquil state. As such, Dameer decided to begin immediately:

"Focus your attention once again on the image of your past self. Tell me what you see and feel."

"He left me, for that I may never forgive him!" Jennifer snapped.

Dameer noted a Eastern European accent. It could have been either German or Austrian. It wasn't unusual for people being regressed to get completely consumed by that life, including taking on an accent.

"Who left you?"

"My physician. I need him. I think I became too dependent on him. He's not a regular physician; he's a mind doctor."

"Take me back in time. Tell me what led you to him in the first place. Do you know who you are?"

"Of course I do! My name's Juliana. Everyone knows me!"

"Why, are you famous?"

"Not in the way you think, not as a performer or an artist. But I'm famous because I'm different."

"How?"

"I come from a very wealthy family. The entire nation knows me. I'm at an age to get married but I don't want to. I've turned down the most eligible bachelors in all of Austria, Spain and Germany!"

"Are you against marriage?"

"Yes, the whole concept disgusts me. Women are made into slaves. It's an institution that benefits men only. I don't wish to become anyone's property, let alone a man's!" Jennifer was obviously completely possessed by this character.

"How else are you different?" Dameer sensed there was more there to uncover.

There was a long pause while Jennifer thought about his question. It was as if she were considering whether or not to disclose some of the information about herself in this life.

"I'm not attracted to men; I like women."

"Go on."

"I'm a beautiful girl. I know that from the constant attention and stares I get from men. But they do nothing for me. I'm not attracted to them at all. I find women's bodies beautiful, so sexy and inviting. I know how to please a woman and they know how to please me."

"Does your family know about your sexual orientation?"

"Are you insane!? They would disown me in a heartbeat! I've already been punished and abused for not agreeing to marry all these wonderful suitors my father brings home! But I'll continue rejecting them … I hate them … I hate them all! They think I'm crazy. I've been a frequent visitor of all the asylums in our area," she said, laughing sarcastically.

"Who thinks you're crazy?"

"My family. It's a great way to get rid of me. They just check me into a mental hospital. They simply say I tried to kill myself again, and they don't have to deal with me for a few months. That's where I met him."

"Met who?"

"My psychiatrist, my mind doctor."

"In one of the asylums?" Dameer asked.

"Yes, at the Bellevue Sanatorium … he is there for me now that my mother's gone. She was the only one who tried to understand me, and I feel so lost without her."

"How did he help you?"

"He helped me deal with the loss of my mother. I gradually began to trust him, and told him more about myself. He's the only one who knows about my attraction towards woman, besides a few of those women themselves of course, and he doesn't think I'm crazy or abnormal.

"He accepts me for who I am and what I feel. He tells me there are many others who feel the same way as I do but I'm just more open to it, that I don't try to deny my desire. He says too many people of our times hide their desires, and that's what makes them insane. He calls it 'repression,' I think."

Dameer thought how applicable this doctor's words were even for today. Too many people live in constant fear of rejection. How sad it is that we must hide our true selves in order to avoid judgment.

"What did you mean when you said he left you?"

"He left just when I thought I was beginning to understand my condition. He's Jewish you see, and was afraid of being persecuted by the Nazis. He moved to England or Italy … I'm not sure, and he never said good bye. I feel so abandoned and alone again."

"I want you to imagine him sitting in front of you once again. Look into his eyes. Do you recognize him from your present life?"

Jennifer took a deep breath and answered in a whisper. "Yes."

"Who is he?"

"It's you."

Amazing! This had never happened before. Dameer needed a few seconds to digest what was taking place. He had been her 'mind doctor' in that life and was reunited with Jennifer in this life to help set things straight.

Dameer felt they should move ahead because she had offered a significant amount of detail already. "Let's move on to the time of your death. Tell me what happened."

"I'm back at home now, and it's so lonely without my mother. I sleep all the time. I have no energy to participate socially, and my father's never around. He locks himself up in his study, drinking all day."

"Do you have a lover?"

"I did … she left me to get married. She said our secret affair was immoral. She broke my heart. I don't think I will ever love another. I don't want to live anymore because I don't belong to this place or time."

"What do you mean?"

"I feel like an outcast, a rebel among conformists. There is a price to pay for defying traditions, culture and religion, and I'm tired of fighting everyone. I'm ready to leave."

"Are you ill?"

"Emotionally, yes … my heart aches. But I'm still quite healthy physically."

"How did you die?"

Suddenly, Jennifer started coughing. She looked like she was suffocating. She placed her hands around her throat and gagged for air.

"I want you to take a few deep breaths. Inhale and exhale as you reach relaxation again. Separate yourself from the scene. Float above it and pretend to be an observer rather than a participant."

It took a few minutes before she felt comfortable to speak again.

"I put on my prettiest dress. It's pink and white and decorated with beautiful embroidery. My hair is braided and I'm wearing make up. I look like I'm getting ready for a wedding. Everyone's out, including the servants."

"What are you preparing for?" Dameer asked, knowing what she was about to say.

"My death."

"How did you die?"

"I hung myself. I tied a rope to a beam across my bedroom ceiling, stood on a chair, put the other end of the rope around my neck and stepped off."

Tears were streaming down her face as she recalled her abrupt passing.

"Tell me what you're feeling."

"I feel so hopeless and alone, so misunderstood. I didn't want to take my life, but I felt living would be harder. My doctor and my mother abandoned me; they left me too soon, when I still needed them.

"I saw no reason to go on. But what a shame. I had so many goals and ambitions. I felt I could change the world … make it a better place for women. Now it's too late."

Jennifer was clearly struggling with the passing of that life. She spent a few more minutes crying and mourning her lost life. She embraced her legs and rocked back and forth as the tears streamed down her face. Even though Dameer felt her pain, he allowed her to go through the motions before intervening. She was exhausted and out of breath.

"Jennifer, can you begin to explain your connection to Austria now?"

She stopped crying and started breathing more normally. Suddenly, she seemed more alert, even with her eyes still closed.

"I left too early, before fulfilling that life's purpose. I was a bundle of confusion and insecurity. I never fully dealt with all the demons haunting me. I chose the easy way out, not realizing that I was only temporarily escaping the problem."

Dameer felt it was time for her to pull back and instructed her to sink deeper into a sleep state. He assured her that the healing process was well on its way and that she would awaken completely rejuvenated. Jennifer lay back down on the hammock, curled up into a fetal position and dozed off.

ﬦﬦﬦﬦﬦﬦ

Adriana

As Dameer sat next to Adriana, he noticed her moving around quite a bit. He felt her restless energy and decided to spend a few minutes helping her to relax again. She responded well to his instructions and gradually sank deeper into a calmer state.

"Try to focus on the image before you. What do you see?"

"It's so green around me. There are hills and valleys as far as the eye can see, and the sun is shining brightly and it's very warm. I'm thirsty."

"Are you walking?"

"I'm looking for my horse. It ran away when my attention was elsewhere."

"Where was your attention. Did something distract you?"

"Something? No not something … she's everything. She's the reason I breathe, the woman of my dreams. I meet her here in the woods once a week. I live for these meetings, and even if the sun and moon spoke to me, I wouldn't notice when in her presence."

Dameer asked Adriana if she knew her name in the life before her.

"Yes, My name is Cyrus."

"Where are you?"

"Persia."

"What year is it?"

"I'm not sure; a different type of calendar comes to my mind than the one you know. But it is long ago."

"Can you describe yourself to me Cyrus?" Dameer asked.

"I'm a very tall and broad-built man, and my hair's brown and long, tied back with a leather strap. I have a beard. I'm wearing some kind of long garment. It's white with layers of other material over it."

"Let's go back to the woman you were talking about earlier. Who is she?"

"She is my twin flame, my other half, the reason I remain alive. She intoxicates my soul with her presence. I never loved like this before and never will. So many women have come and gone, and none can even be compared to her. I don't know if I can ever live without her."

Adriana sounded like she was reciting the most romantic poetry when talking about this mysterious love.

"Why must you meet her secretly?"

"No one knows of our union. She is of common blood, but not to me of course. She is the queen of queens in my eyes, but my family would disown me if they knew, banish me from our land forever.

"I'm of noble blood, and I'm expected to marry nobility. I hate my lineage sometimes. It is the prison that keeps me away from my one and only love."

"What about her family, do they know?"

"No, she must also remain silent about our affair. Her family is very traditional, and they have arranged for her to get married soon. I want to die. I can't imagine existing without her by my side."

Suddenly Adriana's breathing got heavier. She shot up from her hammock.

"What's wrong?"

"I can't bear thinking about another man touching my blossom. She is mine, yet is promised to another. How can fate be so cruel?" She looked agitated and frustrated.

Slowly Adriana rested back down again.

"Remove yourself from the scene if the emotions seem too overwhelming," said Dameer, "I want you to move forward to your love's wedding day. Are you present?"

"Yes."

"Tell me how you feel?"

"She looks so beautiful yet so sad. We met a few days earlier to say goodbye. She ripped out my heart and soul and proclaimed it hers. She cried throughout her wedding.

"Her family thought they were tears of joy; if they only knew. I watched from behind the trees. She didn't know I was there." Adriana looked crushed as she spoke.

"Why did you put yourself through this difficult ordeal?"

"I needed to see it happening. Maybe I never believed she'd go through with it, or maybe I thought she'd see me through the trees and run towards her man and never look back, or maybe I'm a dreamer and the only romantic left in the world."

"What happened after the wedding?"

After a few minutes, Adriana answered softly, "what becomes of anyone without a heart? I died a slow and painful death, yet I was still alive to continue aching. I isolated myself from everyone I loved, family and friends alike. Life lost its taste and beauty as soon as she was gone."

"Gone, what do you mean by gone?"

"She died. He killed her."

"Who?" Dameer realized there was more to the story.

"Her husband."

"Let's go back to that event. Tell me what happened."

"It was all my fault, I should have left her alone, but I had no control over my empty soul and I needed to see her so badly. I asked her to meet me at our secret place near the river, and she agreed."

"Go ahead," Dameer urged, sensing the importance of the next set of events.

"She looks so beautiful ... I want to hold her, kiss her, eat her, but I don't know where to start, and instead I hold back and simply shake her hand and smile.

"We talk under the cherry tree. She tells me about her new life, and she doesn't see me wipe the tears away from my sad eyes," Adriana whispered.

"I want you to look deep into her eyes. Do you recognize her?"

She paused then answered with a smile. "Yes."

"Who is it?"

"It's Stephen. I know she's putting on a brave face. I know she loves me, but I decide to never see her again. She will have no more disturbances from me in her life. I must let go."

So it was Stephen incarnated as Adriana's lover in this life. She would soon be awakened to the realization that he was her soul mate. Listen to that voice within you the next time your lover looks at you in a certain way that sends your heart shattering through your soul, it may be the universe saying she has reunited you once again. The lessons to be learned would soon reveal themselves.

"Did you?"

"Yes, but my promise came too late."

"Why?"

"Her husband had followed us on that day, and he saw everything. He found out about me. I want to kill him ... I swear if I find him I will kill him!!" Adriana was screaming and then burst into tears.

"What did he do to her?"

"I'm not sure exactly. I found out about her death from her brother later. He told me her husband beat her violently when she got home."

"Is that how she died?"

"No ... she died a much worse death."

"Tell me how?"

"He buried her alive ... her family didn't know for days. He later confessed to it. God how she must have suffered those last few hours. I can't bare to think about it anymore!"

"Go to the end of this life. Tell me how you feel."

"I feel so guilty and alone. My love killed her. We should have been more aware of the consequences of our actions, even though what her husband did was evil and wrong. I don't know if I will ever find love again. I only want her, no one else."

"Perhaps you will find her again and your destiny will differ in another life."

Dameer understood now why Stephen was struggling with the decision to leave his family for Adriana. He was fearful of the consequences of that choice. Dameer asked Adriana to briefly relate the events of that life to her present predicament and she expressed the same thoughts Dameer had about Stephen's confusion.

"He thinks that by leaving them, going against everyone's wishes, he might be buried alive again, in some way."

As with Alexander and Jennifer, Dameer allowed Adriana to ponder over the story that had just surfaced. They both remained still for a few moments.

"I'm ready to rest now," said Adriana finally breaking the silence.

‰ℂℒ‰ℂℒ‰ℂℒ‰ℂℒ

Daniel

"Try to clear your mind of all thoughts, sink deeper into relaxation each time you breath in and out. The images of you in your troubled past life surfaces ... look at yourself carefully and tell me what you see." Dameer gently guided Daniel to start.

"I'm in a Godless place," he said sarcastically.

"What do you mean?"

"There is no God here, for God would never create such monsters. These people don't deserve to be among humans on the outside. It smells foul most of the time. There aren't enough rooms for them, and some lie in the corridors for weeks."

Even Daniel's choice of words and sentence construction had changed.

"Do you know where you are?"

"The year is 1785. I'm in France … in a city outside of Paris. I work in an asylum. It's not very big but there are many deranged individuals here."

Dameer was fascinated by Daniel's recollection of details.

"What do you do there?"

"I am a physician, well read on the workings of the body, but the mind still remains a great mystery to me. I ponder the meaning of madness. I'm intrigued by these disturbed individuals."

"What do you mean by disturbed individuals?"

"They are not normal, however it is still unknown as to why they behave in this manner. It may be demons possessing their souls, or perhaps it is the unfortunate severing of the mind from the body. What is clear is that hysteria comes in many forms."

Daniel spoke with such confidence, as if he were the guest speaker at an 18th century medical conference.

"How do you treat these patients?"

"We have various methods, some more successful than others. The deranged are often fearful of us, the physicians."

"Why?"

"Because of the processes employed."

"Tell me about these processes."

Daniel paused, perhaps searching for the right words to describe methods he had no knowledge of in his present life.

"You see, they are mad and therefore need to be treated accordingly. For the severely deranged we employ various restraining devices such as straitjackets attached to the wall, or the patients are strapped into a chair.

"This way they can't harm themselves or my colleagues. At times, they are beaten to try and knock sense back into their minds! Other times we may use baths or showers to help relax them."

Daniel paused again and then spoke in a whisper.

"The lunatics that supposedly hear voices interest me the most. Of course, I don't believe them. Why would a doctor listen to anything a madman has to say … but still, it's fascinating to hear about this imaginary world they claim to be part of."

Dameer decided to direct Daniel to a more specific time or person.

"Tell me about a specific case or patient, someone who claims to hear voices maybe."

"His name is Louise, and he's in his early twenties. He says he hears voices, that they tell him what to do and say, and he fears them immensely. He says he can even see them at times."

"So he has auditory and visual hallucinations?" Dameer asked.

"Yes, that's right. That boy needs to be punished for his lies."

"Why?"

"Some doctors may accept such nonsense, but I don't believe it a bit! These lunatics behave in this manner for attention and have no proof of the ludicrous symptoms they complain about."

"Is he in the asylum still?"

"Yes."

"I'd like you to pay him a visit. Walk towards his room. Tell me, what do you see on the way?"

"I see patients sprawled along the corridors, and they stink of urine and feces. Some are banging their heads on the wall, others just staring out into space. They are disgusting!"

Dameer decided to explore Daniel's resentment towards the patients.

"Why do you despise them so much?"

"They are subhuman, created incomplete, but they don't even try to get better. They just continuously lie about their conditions, making no effort to recover. It frustrates me the most when they blame their actions on hallucinations. They lie ... constantly lie!"

Daniel was convinced that the patients fabricated most of the psychological problems they suffered from. He seemed to feel no remorse or pity. Actually 'hate' would be the perfect descriptor for the emotion he expressed.

"Can you see Louise now?"

"Yes."

"What's he doing?"

"Acting pathetic and mad. He's talking to himself as usual."

"Do you recognize him as someone in your present life?"

Daniel took a deep breath, then answered, "Yes."

"Who is he?"

"Adriana."

"Dameer couldn't have been more pleased. Once again, Rhea had chosen perfectly and invited the searchers with intertwined past incarnations. The wheels of emotional repair were turning in the right direction.

"Have you helped Louise?"

"I thought I had, but his condition just deteriorated."

"Why?"

Daniel suddenly looked anxious.

"Maybe because of the experiments I conducted on him and some of the others."

"Tell me what you did."

"They deserved it!" He looked flustered and upset.

"Deserved what?" Dameer asked gently.

"Everything I did to them!! The shocking, the beating, the solitary confinement, the cages, the operations, all of it! They are ugly creatures that need to be punished!"

"Were you ever questioned, held accountable or punished for your actions?"

"Of course not! I did nothing wrong … anyhow, they would never believe the words of hysterical lunatics."

"What if these ill-fated souls have no control over their behavior?"

Daniel sat back again and pondered Dameer's question.

"Maybe, to a certain extent that is true, but I'm not sure how much of the lunacy is self perpetuated."

"What if it happened to you?' Dameer decided to step out onto the limb a little.

"What rubbish! I'm an educated man, a prominent and respected member of society, a God fearing citizen, and it could never happen to me. Besides, I told you sir, and it seems you don't listen very well, nothing happened to them. They've brought it all on to themselves."

"Take me to the time of your death. What do you see?"

"I'm very old and tired. I devoted too much of my life to work and forgot about living. I died in my sleep with my family around my bed. They don't look too sad as I float away. I don't blame them. They're probably happier with me dead."

"Why do you say that?"

"I wasn't a very nice man. I hurt many people. I would never admit that to anyone, but I feel it necessary to do so right now."

"I want you to sit back and relax again, and to focus on my last question. I want you to think about your actions that went unnoticed and unpunished, think about the resentment and hate you harbor within your heart, and try to imagine the cause of your judgmental and often cruel attitude. Do you think those emotions and actions played a role in who you are in this life?"

"Yes. I now understand what justice means and Karma has a way of enforcing it, even if it occurs in another life. Daniel suffers from visual and auditory hallucinations, the same ailments I refused to accept as genuine symptoms."

Dameer listened as Daniel spoke about himself in the third person, "And believe me, he has no control over it."

Daniel's facial muscles began relaxing as he allowed himself to release the fury and bitterness that had attacked him. Dameer got up from his chair, smiled at Daniel, picked up his folding chair and slowly walked out of the glass enclosure. He felt so content, so honored to be part of such a grand event. Each of his sessions and clients were as important as the next. Each of their journeys had a significant impact on him. He embraced their lessons as his own. He learned from their mistakes, and most of all, he was once again reminded of the endless circle of life. He had every reason to smile.

Dameer walked towards the podium in the middle of the lobby between the hammocks, pressed the lever to lower the glass enclosure and began talking to the four guests in a soft voice:

"Cherish the new images that have surfaced before you today, and as you do, you'll feel even more relaxed. You have begun to understand the importance of these details, and you will become conscious of the fact that even more significance will be brought to light as you awaken and in the days to follow." He paused for a moment before continuing.

"Shortly, I will count from one to ten, and when I reach ten, you'll open your eyes and feel wide awake after your peaceful meditation. You will be invigorated and feel refreshed. Your heart will be filled with understanding and compassion. Clarity will engulf your mind, making you more aware of the reasons you have been experiencing problems in this life."

Dameer started counting, and with each number he gently guided the group back to consciousness. He looked over his shoulder and caught sight of Rhea standing at the far right side of the lobby. She always appeared at this stage. What could be more beautiful than watching four refreshed souls awaken after years of slumber? She stood with her arms crossed and her head tilted, her body present—but her mind miles away, as if dreaming about a lover while watching the sunrise.

ଏଠଔଏଠଔଏଠଔଏଠଔ

The guests ended their meeting with Dameer after sitting in silence for a few moments. Their hammocks swung back and forth, as if to cradle and sooth anxieties resulting from the hypnosis. Dameer answered any questions they had and at this point was always impressed by the amount of detail the seekers usually recalled. Of course there were those who claimed not to remember any aspect of the hypnosis. Some genuinely could not, but Dameer secretly believed some did not want to remember. They chose to block out this experience, as they would block out other issues in life too painful or difficult to deal with.

Unfortunately my dear reader, blocking is not synonymous with vanishing. We may repress thoughts and push them away to what we think are far off places in the mind, yet those contaminated areas of our psyche are closer than we can ever imagine, indirectly affecting our decisions, our experiences and worst of all, surfacing when we least expect it. For that reason, the next time you feel it may be too arduous to address a pressing matter and you feel tempted to exile it from your inner world—please sit down, take a deep breath and grab the dilemma with both hands. Confront it head on and refuse to let it control you from a deeply buried part of your soul. Because that's where blocked thoughts seek refuge, and they will do their best to take revenge if ignored.

After enjoying another marvelous dinner prepared by Adam, Rhea asked her new friends to head to bed after such an exciting day. There was much to reveal, discuss and learn at their meeting in the morning. She instructed them to meet at ten o'clock on the fifth floor of the hotel. The guests were surprised at first, not remembering a fifth floor button on the elevator as they went up to their rooms every night. Rhea quickly clarified their confusion by explaining that the elevator to that floor was located elsewhere. She disclosed its location, wished them a good night and watched them as they walked away.

ଏଠଔଏଠଔଏଠଔଏଠଔ

New Beginnings

"Are you sitting comfortably? Then I'll begin."

—Julia Lang (*Listen with Mother*)

The Last Day …

"Welcome my dear friends," Rhea said, looking more somber than usual.

It wasn't what Rhea was wearing, or the particular way she had styled her hair. It was much deeper than exterior influences. There was something different about her eyes. That morning, the bright twinkle of enthusiasm and charm had abandoned her.

Alexander sat next to Jennifer on the floor; his right arm leaning on her knees while Adriana and Daniel opted for the couch. Chance, Arya, Dameer, Latifah, Adam and Magic were also present, each of them occupying their own corner in that beautiful room, the only room on the fifth floor.

"This seems very serious and official," Adriana whispered to Daniel regarding the mood of the meeting.

"It's true. I don't know what to expect anymore from this bizarre bunch! Just sit back and enjoy the ride," replied Daniel.

"Look at Alexander. He looks like he's about to cry," Daniel continued, whispering back to Adriana, careful not to let Alexander hear. He was through hurting people's feelings.

Alexander did seem miles away. He was quiet and reflective, his head and shoulders slumped lower than his usual graceful and proud posture. In truth, he did not want to leave The Karma Hotel. He did not want this extraordinary experience to end. Still, he felt like a new man and knew more than anything that the last few days had changed him immeasurably.

Rhea suddenly interrupted Alexander's thoughts as she continued speaking.

"I always have very mixed feelings on this day so excuse me if my emotions seem all over the place. On the one hand, I feel a sense of great accomplishment and pride in our endeavor to illuminate the darker, and perhaps somewhat mysterious aspects, of ourselves."

Rhea paused for a second, looked down as if to hide her eyes from her audience, and then went on speaking.

"While on the other hand, I feel a sense of loss and have trouble accepting endings. Not only have we had intimate times together here, but as you now know, I've been following your lives and observing you silently for quite a while.

"So the attachment is greater for me than it is for you. Nevertheless, I must accept change as an inevitable part of life and the growth process. I feel honored to have been part of such an important experience."

Rhea looked back up, making eye contact with each person present in the room.

"My Goodness, what's wrong with me? This sounds like a concluding speech when we haven't even finished!"

"I was going to interrupt you Rhea, to ask you to slow down, but I decided I like it way too much here and really want to keep my job!"

Adam's sudden comment immediately melted the room's tension away as everyone broke out into a comfortable laugh.

"Well, next time, I suggest you do stop me, Adam," said Rhea, winking and half smiling.

It seemed as if the magical twinkle was slowly finding its way back into her eyes.

"Yes, let's continue. As you know, I asked you all to meet my colleagues and me up here on the 5th floor. Previously, you may have thought the hotel only had four floors because the elevator leading to your rooms indicates that.

"You see, the Karma Hotel has many faces to it. Our travelers may be exposed to some of those dimensions, although never all at once, depending on the lessons needed to be learned."

Suddenly, Magic jumped on to Rhea's lap. Rhea pulled the beautiful creature towards her, started stroking his beautiful fur and continued explaining.

"However, the 5th floor is quite common to all those who have come our way, being one of the final areas visited by our guests. This is our center of enlightenment, symbolically located on the highest floor.

"It's where we like to reflect on your journey and the messages that have reached you during the past few days. So without further adieux, let's begin—which will ironically lead to our conclusion."

Rhea put Magic back on the floor, walked towards the center of the room and sat down.

"Could you all join me here please. Let's form a circle and start our dialogue."

The first to join Rhea in forming the circle were Dameer, Latifah, Adam, and Arya, followed by Alexander and Jennifer, and then Adriana and Daniel who closed the circle by sitting in the empty spots left for them.

"You will each have a chance to speak, so please take your time in gathering your thoughts. Let the words find you. Saturate yourself in the experience of feeling rather than trying to rationalize or say 'the right thing.' Let's begin with you Jennifer."

Rhea looked down towards the floor. She looked as if she were praying or in a sudden trance state.

Jennifer's immediate thought was that she felt uncomfortable speaking first. She was caught off guard by the nomination and was hoping to follow suit after one of the others had spoken. Nevertheless, she cleared her mind of fear and anxiety, two emotions that stifle the soul, and began to ponder her recent adventure. After a few moments, she answered in a quiet voice.

"What can I say? My time here has been absolutely incredible. The best way I can describe my feeling is like when you're desperately trying to remember the name of a song. It's on the tip of your tongue, but you can't pinpoint it.

"You can't concentrate on anything else until the name comes to you, and when it does, you have this wonderful sense of relief. Well, for so long I was trying to pinpoint my connection to Austria. I wouldn't say that it completely consumed my world, but the curiosity always remained. You helped me recall the name of my song, if you know what I mean."

Rhea looked at her with pride. "Go on, tell us more."

"I've learned that it's important not to depend on anyone other than yourself for happiness. It's not an emotion that comes from the outside, nor should we seek happiness through others.

"Happiness isn't a permanent state of being either. Some may seek to be happy all the time. I think they're setting themselves up for failure because it comes from special moments we create ourselves throughout life. A certain degree of sadness is necessary. Without sadness, happiness wouldn't nearly taste as sweet."

Jennifer sounded as if she had rehearsed these words for days. Her quiet voice had now risen to a confident pitch. She looked alive and enthusiastic to share her message.

"I think it's so important to express your opinion, views, and life choices without fear of judgment, criticism and worst of all rejection. As long as you're not hurting anyone, you should be ready to stand up for what you believe in.

"And if it's important enough, you'll take on the challenges and sacrifices required to fulfill those dreams. It's not that you're trying to convince or persuade others into buying your ideology. On the contrary, it's about agreeing to disagree. It's about acceptance of the other and the self.

"I think relationships would be so much easier to handle once we stop trying to clone everyone into our perfect mold and embrace people's differences rather than discriminating."

Jennifer took a sip of water, placed her glass back on the floor and continued.

"Of course, time and place are important factors to consider. Expressing your opinion could have cost you your life as early as a century ago."

"That still happens in some parts of the world today," added Daniel.

"True, but it's such a shame for anyone to exist in fear of defining a life for themselves when in reality they are without limitations." She paused. "Like doing a job they think they should rather than one they are interested in; marrying the person they think their family or friends would approve of, rather than waiting for that special someone who will be their true life partner, and constantly using other's opinions, values and expectations to define their own."

Jennifer put her head down, took a few deep breaths and looked back up at her circle of friends.

"Some would rather end a life than change it. I was one of those people. Now I understand that taking your life before the right time only interferes with the universe's grand arrangement. She has a plan for all of us, and both happy and sad moments have been hand-picked, so to speak, to strengthen our soul.

"Committing suicide shows lack of trust and confidence in her plan and it only delays the growth process. That's because we'll have to return once again in another time, repeating the lessons waiting to be learned in the life cut short. I hear she's quite stubborn in that way," Jennifer ended with a smile.

Alexander's thoughts drifted back to his friend Damon. He recalled how similar his words about suicide had been to what Jennifer was saying. Daniel thanked God silently for the fact that he had not actually gone through with killing himself; he could not imagine reliving this life again!

"Beautifully put, Jennifer," Dameer uttered.

Just then, Arya got up from the circle, excused himself and ensured Rhea he would return shortly.

"Thank you, Dameer," said Jennifer, "not only for the compliment, but also for what you did for us. After listening to the tape, and remembering some of the information that surfaced from that life, I realized I'd been given a second chance to meet you in this life."

"That's right. It's quite amazing. I must admit that such an encounter has never happened before," said Dameer, while the others listened intently. "You see, we found out that I was Jennifer's psychiatrist; but we were never able to complete therapy because I moved away to another country due to political reasons, which left her feeling abandoned and even more confused."

"What do you think that means, Jennifer? What might be the significance of meeting Dameer again?" asked Rhea, expertly guiding her towards one of the most important aspects of their discussion.

"I know the rest of you had similar encounters," Rhea continued, "so please ponder this question as well, as it also relates to your own revelations. It's addressed to all of you."

Jennifer was silent for a few moments, looking for the answer.

"I think it's given me a second chance to repair emotional scars and to let go of negative feelings I didn't even know I was carrying."

"I think that discovering the incarnation of a person close to you, coming face to face with that person who hurt you, is a great way to forgive and let go of resentment carried from one life to another," Alexander added to Jennifer's point.

"Kind of like 'making up'—a few hundred years later!" He concluded.

"That's right," agreed Adriana, "as they say, 'better late than never', right?"

"Good, please keep these important ideas in mind," said Rhea, "We will return to them. How about you, Alexander? Please share your thoughts with us."

Rhea focused her attention on him. She knew he had a restless night thinking about his session with Dameer.

Alexander shifted into a cross-legged position. He looked like an important chief addressing his tribe. While listening to Jennifer, his attention shifted from her words to his own thoughts about what he was about to say to the group.

"Thank you Rhea, Chance, Latifah, Dameer, Arya and Adam. I feel as if you've helped reintroduce me to myself, if that makes any sense."

The rest of the people chuckled as Alexander began his reflection.

"My regression to that significant life was astonishing; it touched me in ways I didn't believe possible. I learned that you shouldn't judge someone by the way they look.

"Appearances are only skin deep and God's vision can appear in many forms, shapes and sizes. To be arrogant or put down someone just because of their outer shell would be to insult one of the universe's creations, and who are we to do that?"

Jennifer suddenly felt bad for making fun of people for being too fat, too short, too tall or any other characteristic that set them apart from the norm. She looked at Adriana and sensed that she too was feeling guilty. Both women's thoughts were interrupted as Alexander continued speaking, but the message had sunk in.

"See, what we fail to appreciate is that when a person lacks certain characteristics, physical traits or qualities, more often than not, they are gifted in another way. They may have a special talent or ability that isn't as overt as great hair, for example.

"We need to take time to dig a little deeper; to look past someone with a bad complexion or poor dress sense before deciding whether they interest us or not. The person wearing a hearing aid may have a heart of gold. She may be able to read people in ways unknown to others, and her intuition could be so strong that she's capable of predicting the future!"

Alexander loved every moment of this; never before had he felt more alive and so closely connected to the circle of life.

"You're very right, Alexander. Is that what you experienced as a healer?" Rhea asked.

"Yes, just because I was ugly, didn't get married and was different, all kinds of nasty stuff was said about me. Which leads nicely into what I was about to mention. Gossip! We've all done it and perhaps will still do it without realizing the damage it can cause.

"Gossip can break homes; cause fights, and tear people apart. It is a child of hatred and envy and will stop at nothing. The next time you think you're just having some fun or throwing around harmless words, take a minute to imagine the person you're talking about sitting in the room with you. Would you still continue speaking in the same manner? Would you still tear them apart with your words if you saw their tears falling? I don't think so. I guess what I'm trying to say is that I've learned the importance of weighing my words before throwing them.

"Alexander, you've talked in great detail about what you learned from others' mistakes in that life; what about your own mistakes? Could you tell us a little about that?"

Dameer wanted to make sure he would also voice that part of his enlightenment. After all, this was the core of Alexander's adventure. Alexander paused for a moment and then began speaking in a lower voice.

"I should learn to put my needs before the needs of others. It doesn't make me selfish, but it does protect me from getting hurt unnecessarily. I've come to terms with the fact that I can't save or please everyone all the time, no matter how much I love them. Giving unconditionally and limitlessly to others has drained me."

Adriana gently rubbed his back as he spoke.

"I need to first respect myself and give priority to my needs in order to avoid becoming ill. What good can I be to anyone if I don't take care of myself? Maybe if I become more attentive to myself, others will as well and they will begin to demand less of me.

"Even if I say that I don't have any expectations from those I help, eventually a certain amount of resentment is bound to accumulate within for constantly being the one giving rather than creating an equal situation of give and take."

"That's exactly it. I know it's been difficult for you to accept the latter part of your journey, Alexander; however, it's absolutely essential to your healing process. In order to give, we must all be open to receiving; it's just a part of life. If the receiving or the taking far exceeds the other, then an imbalance occurs," Rhea explained.

"This idea can be applied to any aspect of our lives," explained Chance, "in relationships, between family members, friends or in occupations. As you all know, when doing a reading, the seeker walks away with a part of me, the part in which information about them has come through.

"I could have never continued working all these years if I hadn't learned to replenish that part, to restore the lost energy. Some form of burnout is inevitable when giving limitlessly."

"What about you, Daniel. You've been awfully quiet," commented Rhea.

"I'm listening, I guess, taking in everything you guys are saying," He answered.

"Share your thoughts with us, please," encouraged Rhea.

Daniel looked up at her and smiled. He was surprised by how at ease he felt among these people after such a short time. His thoughts drifted back briefly to Dr. Hartley and how shocked he would be to see one of his most difficult clients engaging so freely with this group of people. He actually felt sad just thinking about parting with them. He decided to be completely honest and without inhibition when speaking.

"I came here not expecting much, to be honest with you. I guess it's because I've been through so many different useless treatments that I thought maybe this would be just another one. My negative outlook on life didn't help either!" he said, laughing for the first time at himself.

"Boy, was I wrong. But I think my experience was different from the others in that the lessons seem to hit me right from the beginning, way before our session with Dameer."

"How so Daniel?' Asked Rhea.

"This might sound a bit odd, but I'll give it a shot anyhow. This whole place and all of you working here seemed so unreal at first. It was like being at a Disneyland for adults. The way it's set up, our rooms, the colors and scents, Magic and of course, the great food … Even you guys," he said looking at Jennifer, Adriana and Alexander, "… seemed so nice and caring.

"I was resistant to accepting it, and I even convinced myself that you were faking the entire 'nice guy' act. But each time I'd see Rhea talking to Latifah, for example, or Adriana spent time with me, I realized that you all were so real and I was the big fake."

Daniel paused for a moment before continuing:

"For the first time in my life I decided to let go of that tough miserable guy who's trying to control me all the time, always telling me how terrible everything about life is and never letting me love, make friends or allowing me to live. Just watching and being with you for the past few days taught me how nice it is to let go.

"To let others into my world without caring if they're going to laugh or judge me. Now I know why I don't have any friends. It's because I didn't want any! Instead of putting my energy and effort into making friends, I used it all up on hating the world for feeling lonely. Does that make sense?" Daniel asked, seeming a little insecure about what he'd said.

"Makes perfect sense, Daniel." Rhea said, radiating with joy at hearing Daniel's introduction.

Indeed, Daniel had come a long way in just a few days.

"I'm glad Dameer's not getting all the credit. We have something to do with all of this too you know!" said Latifah teasingly.

"That's for sure, but my time with Dameer kind of helped complete the picture. Well, maybe not completely. I know I have a long way to go, but knowing who I was in that life and what I did explains a lot.

"Like the hate I had towards shrinks, the reason why I'm haunted by the voices, and most of all, the lack of sensitivity for others. As a psychiatrist in that life, I never fully believed the extent of the patients' illnesses. I could never put myself in their shoes and did not try to empathize with how they felt.

"To be honest with you, up until my time here, I was still doing that in this life. I'd look at fat people with disgust. I'd laugh at people who were disabled, and dumb people would frustrate the hell out of me, and the list goes on and on.

"So I guess, through my condition, the universe, or whoever is in charge of all this madness, is showing me that those poor people in that asylum were really suffering."

"But does life have to be 'madness' Daniel?" asked Dameer.

"I'm sorry, now you know what I mean by still having a long way to go. No, it doesn't have to be. I've created and defined that madness. In the same way, I should be able to create and define a more meaningful life for myself. But sometimes I'm not really sure how."

Daniel put his head down, and for a second, the enthusiasm in what he was saying seemed to lose intensity as he uttered the last words.

Rhea stepped in to pick him back up again.

"You've already started, Daniel. You've redefined the madness by acknowledging that you no longer want to label life as such. That's an incredible achievement.

"The next step is to let go of anger stored up in your soul for so many lifetimes. Release it, discard it, and completely disassociate yourself from it. Rage and resentment do nothing but contaminate our minds. These two emotions stir us away from our soul's purpose, making us behave destructively."

Rhea looked at the others before concluding. "That's something for all of you to think about, not just Daniel."

And Rhea's advice includes you, Dear Reader. Take a minute to think about the people who may have wounded you in your life—and all your lifetimes—causing you anger, resentment and perhaps a bitter taste in

your mouth. Instead of blaming them for hurting you, look at it as a way for them to have emptied their own anger. Those discontented people simply needed an outlet, and you were there, at the wrong time and place. Their misdirected pain should not have an impact on your ability to give, to love and best of all, to heal. Just be selective about who you choose to hand your heart to.

"I wonder what's keeping Arya. He's late," said Rhea.

"Where is he?" asked Jennifer.

"We'll soon find out. We have a little surprise for you," answered Rhea as she looked towards Adriana, "So what about you, Adriana? Tell us how you've been touched."

Adriana got up from her place, walked towards the couch where she had placed her bag, reached in and took out a piece of paper. She walked back to the circle and sat down.

"Last night, after dinner, I went back to my room and listened to the recording of my session with Dameer again. Because I was so moved by the details of that life, I decided to write a little poem, kind of summarizing my feelings. May I read it to you?" She asked the group.

Everyone nodded, eagerly waiting to hear what she had written.

"Please do," said Rhea.

Adriana cleared her throat, took in a deep breath trying to stabilize her quivering voice, and then began to read:

> *My love for you was always certain,*
> *but the distance between us left me confused.*
> *Standing in as a curtain,*
> *those obstacles never allowed us to be fully amused.*
> *They've followed us for years,*
> *They've haunted us for lifetimes.*
> *So many lost tears.*
> *So much lost time, suffering of every kind.*
> *Love keeps bringing you back to me,*
> *even when separated by the vastest sea.*
> *Let's put an end to the separation,*
> *Let's live a life full of aspiration,*
> *Let's seek final retribution,*
> *Let's satisfy love through our eternal unification.*

"I'm not much of a poet. It's my first attempt, to be honest. At least it kind of rhymes, right?"

Adriana was obviously nervous about her audience's reaction.

"I love it. It's beautiful!" cried Alexander.

Adriana smiled shyly as the others also joined Alexander in giving her praise. She folded her poem carefully and placed it in the side pocket of her jeans. She thought about Stephen and if he would be as touched as the others to hear her words. After all, the poem was written for him.

"I agree with the others. Your words are so genuine and moving. You ought to write more often," added Rhea, "Now that you have our full attention, tell us about your journey; what did you stumble upon on the way?"

Adriana took a deep breath, bit her lower lip, then began to answer softly.

"I learned about the word 'love'. I mean, we all think we know what love is, but not enough people understand its true depth or power. Including me, up until yesterday.

"People claim to be in love all the time. But what they don't understand is that true love comes without judgment or conditions. True love should be about complete acceptance of the other person, not a situation wherein we like a few of our partner's characteristics and think that we can or should change the ones we don't. I chose the wrong person on a few occasions, while under the false impression that I could somehow mold them into that perfect man of my dreams. Needless to say, those relationships didn't last very long, because trying to change someone only leads to frustration and resentment."

Adriana fell silent for a moment, and then began to speak again.

"Last night as I lay in bed, it suddenly dawned on me that if I have this dream lover in my mind, then surely he must have me in his mind. Isn't that what soul mates are about, souls being separated at birth only to be reunited by love? Suddenly all the hurt and anger about past relationships that failed had faded away."

Her tone became firmer.

"Clarity hit me like a tornado! You see, those relationships didn't fail. They were just never meant to be. It is the universe's way of trying to clear the path for our soul mates to find us.

"If we resist her plan by staying in an unfulfilling union, then we end up bitter, angry at the world, anxious and sometimes we even stop believing that true love really exists.

"But if we surrender to her by letting go of an unhealthy relationship, by loving ourselves enough to set high expectations of how we should be treated, then love will find us, and what a heavenly reunion that will be. Believe me, I know."

"What about times when the person seems to be perfect but there are so many obstacles in the way of true love?" Jennifer questioned.

"Of course, each situation has different factors influencing the relationship, so I'll speak about the lessons I've learned along the way. People come into our lives for different reasons. Sometimes we are meant to learn from them, while other times, we act as the teachers. Those relationships are important, because they prepare us for our true-life companion."

"Precisely Adriana, and if I may add," said Rhea, "usually what happens in unequal relationships, in terms of learning and growth, is that people come together from two different dimensions, relating to one another on different wavelengths.

"But the most important reason Fate brings them to us is that those individuals help us identify that perfect lover we all hold so close to our hearts. After all, how can you know what you like or don't like about someone if you haven't experienced differences?"

"I understand completely! It's like asking someone who's never tried shellfish if they like oysters. They won't know until they've tried them. Only then can they make up their mind about our little sea friends," Adam said, relating the conversation to his own passion: food!

"Adam, you're so silly!" said Latifah, giggling with the others.

As the laughing died down, Chance continued where Rhea had left off.

"I think there are two types of obstacles in a relationship; obstacles related to character and obstacles related to life circumstance. The first type is the most difficult to overcome or resolve because essentially what you're trying to do is to alter the essence of a person. Resolution might be possible, but more often than not, it's only short term and the person being changed will soon bounce back into their old habits. And they have every right to do so! After all, why should they change? How wonderful it would be if they could find a person who would accept and more importantly love them exactly as they are."

Chance took her floppy old hat from off the floor and placed it on her head.

"See, now if any guy ever told me never to wear this hat again, I'd show him the door, real quick!" Chance said, making light of her point, but the message was loud and clear.

"Think about it. If someone would love you only after they have changed you, then it's no longer 'you' they are in love with."

"What do you mean by obstacles related to life circumstance?" asked Alexander.

"I mean things such as deciding where to live, trying to convince your dad that he or she is the one, deciding on what car to buy, who does what at home, trying to get your partner interested in some of your hobbies or what school the kids should go to. Basic things that can be ironed out through compromise," ended Chance.

"So, the obstacles don't matter too much when you're in a relationship that's not meant to be," said Adriana, "I never exerted too much energy in trying to make it work. I imagine those who do only end up getting hurt, feeling disappointed and rejected.

"But once Fate blesses us with our soul mate, no obstacles in the world can stop us from staying with each other. Of course, with the will and determination of the ones who adhere to love. I don't think love comes to those who are blinded by fear or aren't ready for it."

Adriana stopped for a brief moment, drank out of her cup and then continued to speak.

"I think I've been fortunate enough to have found my other half. I questioned that endlessly, because of the obstacles in our way, but the session with Dameer confirmed everything my heart was trying to tell me.

"I just wasn't listening. I was constantly allowing my thoughts to be clouded over by society's expectations and definitions, of how and what a relationship should be like. I tried convincing myself endlessly to let go of Stephen, to find another man and form a normal relationship.

"But I just couldn't. Something keeps bringing me back to him, a force so great that it could only be called true love or destiny. In that lifetime, which was only one of the times I know of our union, and Dameer said we could have met during many other incarnations, I didn't fully appreciate the gift of love. I didn't fight for what I believed in.

"The expectations from my family were so overwhelming that I chose the easy way out. I let go of the one person I loved so deeply in order to keep everyone else happy, meanwhile killing him and myself in the process."

"What do you think is the biggest obstacle in your way of being with Stephen in this life?" asked Chance.

"Well, other than his wife and children, I think it's the fear of change and the consequences of divorce that holds him back. He's admitted to not being in a happy marriage, but for some reason he still remains locked inside it.

"He might be carrying the fear of being killed, as he was in that life, if he were to choose me. Perhaps not literally killed, but he may fear a kind of symbolic death or rejection from the people around him. I really don't know anymore what he thinks.

"If things are meant to work out, they will. I need to surrender to Fate and the universe; they'll show me the way. But I'm certain of one thing; I've never been as in love with anyone as I am with Stephen, never."

"Are you sure, Adriana?"

Suddenly, Adriana jumped as if she had heard a ghost. She turned her head, looked behind her and found Stephen standing next to Arya. Was this a dream?

'Oh God please don't wake me up if this is a dream!' She thought, darting her attention back to Rhea for some kind of clarification.

"Welcome Stephen. I'm so pleased you could make it," said Rhea, smiling with tears in her eyes.

Adriana flew from where she was sitting and ran towards Stephen. He grabbed her in his arms, stroking her hair as she cried like a helpless child. She took his face in her hands repeatedly, kissing him as reassurance that he was really there.

"Thank you, Rhea. It's my pleasure. I'd go to the ends of the Earth if I had to for this girl," Stephen whispered softly, "I was so worried about you when you just disappeared without a trace. It made me realize just how much you mean to me. I thought I'd lost you Adriana, and that drove me insane. I never want to lose you again. Never."

"You'll have the rest of the afternoon to catch up with one another. I know you have a lot to talk about. Please join us now in the last part of our passage," Rhea said, "All of you please sit next to the person who was present in the life you visited. Look them straight in the eyes and either ask them for forgiveness or tell them that you have forgiven them for what happened.

"Letting go of that anger is key to clearing your karma, no matter how difficult it may seem. Forgiving is an act to help repair our soul since every time we think about how others did us wrong, we continue pouring salt into those open wounds."

"What about the people we hold resentment towards in this life, Rhea?" questioned Alexander.

Rhea paused a moment before answering. This was not usually part of the final stage, but what an ingenious idea, she thought. Trust Alexander to be the one to come up with that idea!

"That's a great suggestion, Alexander. Once you have spoken to your partners, please sit by yourself and meditate for a while on those who caused you pain or heartache in this life. Visualize them in your thoughts, think about what they did, and finally release yourself from the grasp of hate and blame."

Rhea stood up from the circle, allowing the others to move around into the appropriate position. She watched how they communicated, how they touched and held one another. Beautiful words of apology were exchanged, words of gratitude expressed, and tears streamed down their faces, as if to wash away all the sorrow and pain carried around for so many lifetimes. She watched as the look of life and love flowed back into their faces. Eventually, each guest sat alone in different areas of the room and began meditating on the past, the present and the dazzling future waiting to be written. *After all, we each are the authors of this beautiful story called 'life.'*

☙☗☙☗☙☗☙☗

Dear Reader,

The last chapter is called 'New Beginnings' for a reason. There are no endings and life should not be treated as such. There are only lessons to be learned, to arm us for new experiences that the endless circle of life brings forth. Even when you say goodbye to a lover whom you may never see again, think about the way the reminiscence of their face, the sound of their laugh, the echo of their soul remains forever etched in our memory. The images may slightly fade, but they never completely disappear.

You have been witness to the exploration process of four souls looking to make better sense of life's trials and tribulations. But as you hold me in your hand and turn the last pages of my voice, I feel your sense of connection and understanding. You were not mere spectators to Adriana, Jennifer, Daniel and Alexander's journey. You traveled side by side, each of them. Their stories became your stories; their lessons and experiences were added to your spiritual growth process and most important of all, you helped me accomplish my mission by putting a smile on your face and occasionally warming your heart.

I will silence my whispers for now, but this will not be the last time we meet. Fate will bring us back together again. Until then I leave you with 'The Four Immeasurable Thoughts' put forth through the Buddhist Philosophy:

> **'May all beings have happiness & the cause of happiness**
> **May all be apart from sorrow & the cause of sorrow**
> **May all not be apart from the bliss that is sorrowless**
> **May all leave attachment & hatred towards those near & far by living**
> **in equanimity.'**

Love,
This Book

About the Author

Samineh Izedi Shaheem is an assistant professor of Psychology at the American International University in London where she teaches a wide range of courses including Introduction to Psychology, Cross Cultural Psychology, Pathologies and I/O Psychology. She is Canadian but from a Middle Eastern background (Iranian) and has studied and worked in different parts of the world, including The United Sates of America, The Netherlands, The United Arab Emirates and of course London.

Samineh is also one of the featured writers of *All Women Magazine*, which is distributed throughout the Middle East. She has a very unique monthly column and problem page focusing on the diverse cultural character of that region. Readers write their issues/concerns in and she tries to the best of her ability to guide them in the right direction.

Samineh takes her role to educate our future generation very seriously, and aims to reach as many individuals who may require guidance during the trying stages of their educational period and throughout life in order to make a difference in people's lives. By engaging in both writing and lecturing, Samineh believes she is able to use these two mediums of communication in order to assist individuals in having more meaningful experiences and clarity throughout life.

Author Photograph © 2007 Le Studio Mystique (Dubai).

978-0-595-47945-0
0-595-47945-6

Lightning Source UK Ltd.
Milton Keynes UK
UKOW04f2014140214

226491UK00001B/224/P